Molly stopped herself. Why was she gabbling like this? Why not tell him what she really wanted to say? 'I thought about you today,' she admitted.

Frank was delighted. 'You did?'

'Yes. I mean, seeing you again. I mean, well, you know, seeing you again after so many months.'

'Yeah. Funny.'

'Yes.'

There was another pause while they studied each other's faces more closely. Frank loved the curve of her cheek.

I'm married, too,' he confessed.

'Well, lots of people are.'

'Yeah, I guess so.'

They exchanged another smile . . .

Falling in Love

A novel by
KENNETH HARPER

from the screenplay by
MICHAEL CRISTOFER

PANTHER
Granada Publishing

Panther Books
Granada Publishing Ltd
8 Grafton Street, London W1X 3LA

Published by Panther Books 1985

Copyright © Paramount Pictures Corporation 1985

ISBN 0-586-06682-9

Printed and bound in Great Britain by
Collins, Glasgow

Set in Times

Chapter 1

Westchester County awoke to find the sun shining with benign authority out of a bright blue sky. In the clean, crisp December air, everything seemed to stand out with remarkable clarity and colours were intensified to their deepest hues. Bare trees took on vivid life, empty fields were filled with simple wonder, farms smiled. In the towns themselves the effect was equally dramatic. Houses were freshly painted, shop windows polished, roads resurfaced, cars washed.

The Hudson River Valley blossomed most of all in the winter sunshine. Shimmering in the brilliant glare, the mighty waterway flowed on with calm sense of purpose between twisting banks that rose and fell and provided endless perspectives on breathtaking scenic beauty. As always, Nature was her own best lighting designer.

The train saw none of the spectacular landscape.

A long, gleaming, elegant monster with blue and silver scales, it glided at speed towards New York City along the east side of the river and ignored the view completely. It had done the journey so often that even the extraordinary had become commonplace. The passengers, too, had other things to think about. They were commuters, heading for their workplaces in the city, still wiping the sleep from their eyes, getting themselves ready for another day at the office or factory or store. Some read, some smoked, some talked, some did crosswords. But there was a corporate sense of resignation.

They were one small part of the huge suburban workforce that came into Manhattan to earn its keep. They were there because they had to be. Their expressions were vacant and noncommital.

Molly Gilmore was different.

As she waited for the train to reach Ardsley Station, her face was serene and untroubled. A handful of people waited with her, standing on fixed spots like so many statues, staring blankly into space. Molly strolled casually along the platform. She checked her watch, tucked her handbag more firmly under her arm, then noticed the way that the sun was glinting on the track.

Molly Gilmore was a tall, slim, handsome woman in her thirties. She had long, lustrous auburn hair which she wore in a variety of styles depending on her moods, and she favoured loose-fitting clothes. The hair was up at the moment and a pale fawn coat had been chosen for the day's outing.

She was not a typical commuter. What set her apart from the other passengers was the fact that she was looking forward to her trip. They had all switched to automatic pilot and were simply following a daily routine. Molly was not. For them, Manhattan was a kind of prison: for her, it was a means of escape.

The train came around a long, graceful bend in the track and then straightened up as it headed for the station. Molly glanced at the circled letter M as it surged towards her on the front of the train. When the doors slid open to let them aboard, she flicked an eye at the name emblazoned on the side of the car – Metro North Commuter Railroad. She was no sooner inside than the doors closed behind her and the train resumed its journey.

Molly went down the aisle between the seats and found herself a place on the right. A few muted conversations were in progress but it was the general air of grim acceptance that still pervaded. The freedom and cleanliness of Westchester County was being traded for the frenzied bustle of workaday Manhattan.

Except in the case of Molly Gilmore.

She sat there quietly and went through the list of things to be done, putting them in order of priority. She had to ring Brian. Tell him about the car. Do some Christmas shopping. Grab something to eat. Do some more shopping. Meet a friend. Visit her father. Make a last round of the shops. Then ride the train home.

It was a hectic schedule but Molly did not mind that. In fact, she was certain that she was going to enjoy it. However exhausting it might be, it sure beat staying alone in the house all day.

The train thundered on. Outside the windows, many other striking views flashed past unseen. It was carrying an army of the blind.

A minute before the train arrived at Dobbs Ferry, a taxi screeched to a halt outside the station and the lean figure of Frank Raftis leaped out. Carrying a briefcase and some rolled-up drawings, he was wearing a green trench coat and the look of a man in a hurry. The usual rugged charm of his features was obscured by a frown of anxiety.

Frank pushed money at the cab driver.

'This is too much,' admitted the man.

'Keep it. Keep it.'

'Sure. Thanks . . . oh, and Merry Christmas!'

But Frank had already raced into the station.

When the train pulled up alongside the platform, the dozen or so commuters came to life long enough to step into it. Frank had to run fast and jump quickly before the sliding doors closed behind him. He sighed with relief and then strode down the car in search of a seat. As he flopped down beside another man, he did not notice that the woman sitting immediately in front of him had lovely auburn hair. He was too preoccupied with other matters

7

and with running a hand through his own close-cropped black hair.

Frank went through his own list. Ring up about the car. Call in at the office. Do some Christmas shopping. Grab a bite around mid-morning. Do some more shopping. Meet Ed for lunch. Check back with the office. Force himself into a final spending spree on presents. Then ride the train home.

He did not relish the punishing schedule. It made him feel tired before he had even started. Looking around the car, he realised why he preferred to drive into the city.

He sat back and closed his eyes for a few minutes.

When the train finally arrived at Grand Central Station, its passengers poured out on to the platform and headed for the escalators. Molly Gilmore was carried along by the thrusting mass of people. Not far behind her was Frank Raftis, trying to prevent his drawings from being squashed in the throng.

Other trains with other hordes of commuters were arriving at the terminal at regular intervals and the main concourse was a sea of anonymous faces. Molly pushed her way towards a battery of telephones. When she put a coin into the machine, she did not notice that the man in the adjoining booth was wearing a green trench coat that was unbuttoned down the front.

Frank got through at precisely the time that Molly did. Standing less than a yard apart, they took part in telephone conversations that seemed to overlap. Both had to shout to make themselves heard above the din of the passing multitudes.

'Hi. It's me,' yelled Frank. 'Car problems . . .'

'Hello. Dr Gilmore, please. Yes, I know. Uh . . . this is his wife . . . Yes. Hi . . . No, I can't. I'm in a phone booth.'

'Just tell them to go ahead and fix it.'

'No, I'm in the city,' explained Molly.

'I'm in New York.'

'Yes.'

'Yes.'

'Well, no . . .'

'Not really . . .'

'Tell him the car wouldn't start so I took the train.'

'No, I took the train . . . Yeah. Alright?'

'OK?'

'OK.' replied Frank. 'How are you?'

'I'm fine . . .'

'Good.'

'Merry Christmas.'

'Yeah, Merry Christmas to you, too.'

'Bye . . . Thanks. Bye . . .'

'OK. Bye . . .'

They put down their respective receivers and left their booths. Their paths crossed briefly as they aimed for different exits. While Molly came out through one door and hailed a taxi, Frank emerged from another and flagged down a vehicle for himself.

Still unaware of each other's existence, they were driven to their separate destinations through congested streets. Manhattan was busier and noisier than ever. Christmas had brought out the brass bands and Santa Claus appeared on almost every other corner. Molly's cab driver cursed at the choking traffic while Frank's vented his spleen on the festive season itself.

Both passengers were glad to pay their fare and get out.

Molly was on Fifth Avenue. She looked up at her first port of call, took a deep breath, and plunged on in. The store was heaving with people and positively ablaze with multi-coloured Christmas decorations. Simply reaching certain items in order to examine them was a problem. Getting served was sometimes in the nature of an ordeal.

But Molly persevered. Showing good humour and saintly patience, she kept at it until she had collected half a dozen bags of gifts. Then she fought her way back to the main door and came out to the welcome slap of cold air. She moved slowly along the sidewalk, glad to have escaped the punitive central heating of the store. She had walked a block or so before she had cooled down.

Rising majestically above the chaos was St Patrick's Cathedral, its twin towers soaring to a height of over three hundred feet, its Gothic stonework and stained glass windows giving it a startling uniqueness among the concrete skyscrapers. High above her, Molly could hear the cathedral bells chiming the hour. She was reminded just how long it was since she had last eaten.

A Sabrette hot dog trolley was standing on the corner. She walked past it, stopped, considered, then went back. One long, sustained bout of shopping had helped her to work up an appetite.

'Could I have a hot dog?' she asked.

'Sure thing,' said the vendor, obligingly.

'Just mustard.'

'No relish, no chili, no onions?'

'Just mustard.'

'It's Christmas,' he urged. 'Treat yourself.'

Molly smiled. 'Just mustard.'

'You got it.'

A hot dog with just mustard was duly handed over. Molly put all the bags into one hand so that she could hold it. The snack was hot and filling. It revived her for another assault on the stores.

With an identical hot dog and an identical problem of how to eat it and carry his shopping bags at the same time, Frank Raftis jostled his way towards the bank of elevators on the main floor of Saks Fifth Avenue. The whole place had been transformed into a winterland of white branches

10

and white Christmas lights. It was all lost on Frank. His eyes were firmly fixed on the indicator panels above the elevator.

A light came on, a bell pinged and the elevator doors parted. As soon as the occupants had come out there was a competitive rush from new passengers. Frank was among the last to press himself inside before the metal doors closed behind him with a dull thump. He put the hot dog in his mouth, transferred all the bags to one hand, then used the other to fish out a shopping list. He glanced up as a woman began to press buttons on the control panel.

He spoke through a mouthful of hot dog.

'Four, please.'

'I beg your pardon?' she said.

He removed the hot dog. 'Would you press four? Fourth floor.'

'Oh. No.'

'What?'

'No, it doesn't,' she explained, turning to him.

'I want the fourth floor,' he persisted.

'You shouldn't be eating in here.'

'I know . . .'

'Think of our clothes,' she reproached.

'Look, would you just press that button there?' he asked, nodding towards the panel. 'The one that says four.'

'Sure. But it won't stop there.'

'Why not?'

'This is an express.'

She was right. About his eating. And about the elevator.

Without any intermediate stops, it rocketed to the top floor and came to a surprisingly gentle halt. Frank went guiltily off to a corner to finish the hot dog then he took his bearings before heading for the escalator. As he

11

descended on the moving stairway, he looked around at the maelstrom below him. How could anybody actually *enjoy* Christmas shopping? It was like going over an assault course in sub-tropical temperatures. There had to be an easier way. Next year, maybe, he would do it all by mail order.

As one escalator carried him down, another was taking Molly Gilmore up. They passed each other yet again without being conscious of the fact. Both were concentrating on the job in hand.

'This one is very nice . . .'

'Yeah.'

'On the other hand, this one has more character.'

'I can see that . . .'

Molly was in a dilemma. She had to choose between a plain woollen cardigan and a bright, colourful pullover. The cardigan was safe and conservative and Brian would definitely wear it. With the pullover, she would be taking more of a chance because her husband's attitude to clothing was one of great caution. Logically, it had to be the cardigan but something inside her preferred the pullover. It was high time that she changed Brian's image as a staid dresser.

'You could always take them both,' suggested the salesgirl.

'That way, he'd only wear one of them.'

'Which one?'

'This one,' decided Molly, holding up the cardigan. Her mind was made up. 'I'll take the pullover.'

She searched in her bag for her purse.

While Molly Gilmore was coming to her decision up in the Men's Department, Frank Raftis was still trying to reach his down in the Women's Department. His choice lay between a very scanty, exotic negligee and a sensible pale blue bathrobe. The saleswoman tried to help him.

'If it was *my* husband he'd go for this,' she confided, pointing to the negligee. 'He'd say it was more feminine.'

'Oh yeah. It is.'

'What sort of person is your wife?'

'How do you mean?'

'Which one would *she* buy?'

Frank lifted up the bathrobe. Ann would never buy anything as revealing and inviting as the negligee. She dressed to suit herself and not her husband. Perhaps it was time she became a little more adventurous. Frank put the bathrobe aside.

'I'll take the negligee . . .'

'Your wife will be thrilled,' she assured him.

'I hope so . . .'

He paid for it then added one more parcel to a fast-growing collection. Out came his list again. The children. They were his next priority. He left the store and strode up Fifth Avenue.

Molly came out a few minutes later and headed in the same direction. Her feet were starting to feel the strain and the weight of her packages was now appreciable but she consoled herself with the fact that she had broken the back of the shopping. One more store and then it would be time to meet up with Isabelle. The thought gave her the incentive to press on.

As she passed a shop window, something caught her eye and made her stop. A display of children's sporting goods filled the window and she gazed at it wistfully. At Christmas more than at any other time, she missed having children to buy for and please and love. She found herself wondering yet again what sort of a mother she would have been and how Brian would have shaped up as a father. But it was not to be.

Her reverie was interrupted by a man who climbed into the window to reach one of the items on display. Though their eyes met for no more than a split second, she felt suddenly embarrassed, caught off guard during a very private moment. Tightening her grip on her bags, she hurried along the sidewalk.

The salesman, meanwhile, stepped back into the shop and handed the baseball bat to the customer. Frank Raftis judged its weight then took a few practice swings.

'It's fine.'

'Then you'll take it, sir?'

'No. I'll take two.'

'Two?'

'I'm ambidextrous.'

'Oh, I see,' noted the salesman uncertainly.

'I got two sons. And that means two baseball bats.'

'Ah!'

The man understood now and produced a mirthless laugh.

While the man wrapped the gifts, Frank checked his list once more. There was still a long way to go. He opted for a last foray before rewarding himself with a well-earned rest. It would be a treat to take the weight off his legs in the company of a close friend.

Ed Lasky was seated at a booth in the restaurant.

'Frank! Over here!'

'Hi, Ed . . .'

'What kept you?'

'Shopping,' said Frank, sinking gratefully down on his chair. 'Going around just about every store on Fifth Avenue.'

'What the hell for!'

'It's Christmas Eve, Ed. Christmas Eve.'

'Jesus Christ.'

'That's the spirit!'

Ed Lasky was a well-built man of middle height with a round open face and thinning hair that was swept straight

14

back from his high forehead. The eyes had a cynical twinkle in them and the nose looked as if it might have done service in a boxing ring. Though he was roughly the same age as his companion, he seemed much older and tireder. Frank slapped him warmly on the shoulder.

'How are you?'

'Lousy. How are *you*?'

'Fine. Life is terrific!'

'What are you, crazy?'

'No, I'm not crazy, Ed. I just feel good, that's all. It's Christmas Eve. My car broke down this morning, I got in late, I missed two appointments, and I just spent a fortune buying the wrong gifts for everyone.' He grinned broadly. 'I feel great! How's Susan?'

'We're getting a divorce.'

It was a casual remark accompanied by Ed's usual shrug but it shook Frank. He did not know what to say. At that moment, a waitress came up to the table and handed him a menu.

'Would you like a drink?' Her voice was a flat monotone.

'No, what? Oh yeah.' He was still trying to take on board the idea of divorce between Ed and Susan. 'Uh. Something. What? A beer. I'll have a beer.'

The waitress reeled off the possibilities.

'Heineken, Michelob, Molson, Becks, Bud, Coors, Tuborg, Miller, Miller Light, Schlitz, Guinness, Carlsberg or Lowenbrau.'

'Yeah. Anything.'

'Gimme a break, will you?' she pleaded.

'Uh. Miller. Miller Light.'

'OK.'

'Make that a Schlitz!' he called after her.

'On its way . . .'

As the girl crossed to the bar, Ed appraised her carefully. 'No face. Great body. Passive. Waitresses are always

15

passive. It's rough on the elbows.' He saw the concern in his friend's face and mistook it for reproach. 'A guy is entitled to eye the cheese.'

'Ed. Susan.'

'Oh. That.'

'Yeah. *That*.'

'Well. It's no big deal.' Again, the characteristic shrug. 'It was coming. I've been seeing Carol over a year. It's no secret. I figured the kids, you know, all that. So we stuck it out. This is better. It's honest. At least.' He manufactured a smile. 'Merry Christmas.'

'I'm sorry,' murmured Frank.

'You are?'

'Yeah. I guess.'

'Why?'

'I don't know.'

But Frank did know. Divorce meant pain and bitterness. Ed and Susan had been married long enough for that pain to be intense and that bitterness to be corroding. It was like hearing about the death of someone you love. A marriage had passed away and a part of Frank was in mourning. He sensed that Ed, for all his outward indifference, was in mourning as well.

Frank reached out and put a comforting hand on his arm.

'Merry Christmas!' replied Ed with heavy irony.

The waitress came back with the beer.

Time spent with Ed Lasky was never less than entertaining and a lot of laughs were shared over the meal, but Frank still got up from the table with a residual sadness. Ed and Susan. He had been at their wedding. Their christenings. Their parties. Everything. Ed and Susan Lasky. Of all people. It was too close for comfort.

They left the restaurant and came out into the street.

'How's Ann?'

'Oh. She's in great shape.'

'Bought her something nice?'

'I sure hope so, Ed.'

'Susan always hated my Christmas presents. If I bought the right size, it was the wrong colour. If I bought the right colour, it was the wrong style. Women!' He waved a hand expansively. 'All over. I got no more worries on that score. Don't need to buy Susan a goddam thing ever again!'

'Ed. Is there no chance . . .?'

'We blew it. Now forget it, will you?'

'Yeah.'

'And give Ann a kiss from me.'

'I will . . .'

They shook hands and parted. Frank strolled in the direction of Rockefeller Plaza and it was not long before he heard the sound of the choir rising above the pandemonium of the traffic. They were singing 'O Come All Ye Faithful!' and they were in good voice.

As he went off to listen to them properly for a few minutes, he passed two women who were walking arm in arm and clearly enjoying each other's company. Frank gave them no more than a cursory glance and they did not even register his presence. Molly Gilmore and her best friend were far too deep in conversation to notice anybody. They laughed aloud like schoolgirls exchanging stories about their sexual experiences.

'So where are you going, Isabelle?'

'Acapulco. Monday morning.'

'Who with?'

'David.'

'Which one is David?'

'The young one.'

'They're all young ones!' giggled Molly.

Isabelle was a shorter, darker woman in her thirties

17

with an almost permanent smile and a mischievous eye. She loved to tease and shock her more conventional friend.

'The *young* young one,' she explained. 'I told you about him.'

'I don't remember.'

'Yes, you do.'

'I don't, Isabelle. Unless it was David from Montclair.'

'That was *ages* ago, darling!' corrected the other. 'This David is much nicer – and much younger. He's gorgeous. Dark hair. Big eyes. From the gym. I told you, Molly. The one with the ass.'

Everything became clear. 'Oh, *that* David.'

'That ass could win prizes! So could something else.'

They laughed together for a dozen yards or more.

'How long will you be gone?' wondered Molly.

'Until New Year's Day. Barry's family is coming in.'

'Barry?'

'That's what I said.'

'*The* Barry?'

'Yeah. We have this dinner every year. Well, he's still my husband, sort of. And it's important to him. So . . .'

'You're terrible!' said Molly, smiling.

'Listen,' countered the other. 'I was faithful for ten years. I have a lot of catching up to do. We can't *all* be happily married.'

'Do you think you ever were?'

'What?'

'Happily married.'

'Oh yes. I was, I was . . .'

They walked on in silence for a while. Isabelle seemed pensive. She soon discarded her thoughts and turned back to her friend.

'How's Brian?'

'He's fine.'

18

'You haven't mentioned him so far.'

'He never came up.'

'Still the perfect husband?'

'I've got no complaints,' returned Molly, easily.

'You're getting self-satisfied!'

'Am I?'

'Besides, I don't believe there *is* such a thing as a perfect husband. Contradiction in terms.' They stopped outside a huge office building. 'Don't you wish you could come with me?'

'Into the office?'

'No. To Acapulco.'

'David might not like it.'

'You know what I'm saying, Molly. Don't you envy me? A little?'

There was a pause. 'I've got to go, Isabelle.'

'Me, too. I'll call you when I get back.'

'You can show me your tan.'

'I'm not going down there for a tan, honey! Bye!'

Isabelle went up the steps to the entrance.

'Merry Christmas!' called Molly.

'What?'

'Never mind!'

Molly Gilmore was soon lost in the crowd. It was several minutes before she dared to answer the question that her friend had put to her. Yes. She did envy Isabelle. Just a little.

There really was no such thing as a perfect husband.

Chapter 2

John Trainer sat in the window of his luxury apartment on Fifth Avenue and gazed down affectionately at Central Park. The afternoon sun gave it a stark beauty, emphasizing the splendour of its woodland and its generous expanses of green grass, turning its lakes and ponds into glittering blue mirrors of crystal. Ducks scudded across the placid water. Birds flew in profusion. Walkers, joggers, cyclists and children were dotted about everywhere. Skaters laughed and waved as they circled around the ice rink. There was even a lone tourist trying to take a photograph of the statue of Hans Christian Andersen.

Central Park was having its own Christmas celebrations.

John Trainer lowered his eyes. A big, heavy man in his sixties, he was wearing slacks, shirt and woolly cardigan. His face was drawn, his skin pale. There was a listless quality about him. He picked at his moustache and then raised his eyes to inspect the view once more. It was as special to him as it had always been. He had chosen the apartment because of its prospect. Central Park never let him down.

The thought of losing it made his stomach lurch.

From the distant hallway came the sound of the doorbell and of feet scurrying across the thick carpet. The door was opened and muffled voices could be heard. After a few moments, Molly Gilmore came into the room. She walked straight across to her father and gave him a kiss on the forehead.

'Hello, killer.'

'Where the hell have *you* been?' he demanded.

'Shopping. How are you?'

'If you weren't so beautiful, I wouldn't have waited,' he told her. 'Give me another kiss.'

Molly obliged. 'Now answer my question. How are you?'

'Fine. Just back from a run round the park.'

'Be serious.'

'You know me. I'm never serious on an empty stomach. Come on. Lunch has been waiting for the last hour.'

With visible strain he began to rise from the chair.

'Let me help you,' she offered, taking his arm.

'I can manage,' he insisted. 'I'm not an invalid.'

'Of course not . . .'

As they went through into the dining room, she noticed how slowly he was walking but she made no comment. They settled down at one end of the long, polished mahogany table and he rang a small copper bell. A small, neat, bustling middle-aged woman came in at once.

'Yes, Mr Trainer?'

'Food.'

'Right away . . .'

The woman disappeared into the kitchen but came back almost immediately with the first course on a tray. Molly tucked into her soup with relish but her father only toyed with his. The woman came in to clear the plates away then served the main course from a trolley which she wheeled in. Though he was only given small portions of everything, Molly's father still did not clear his plate. She was worried about him. In the past, he had always been very fond of his food and willing to try almost any dish set in front of him.

Throughout the meal, she kept the conversation to such neutral subjects as the weather, the Christmas traffic and the state of the dollar. Only when they had finished eating did she get around to more personal matters. He had relaxed a lot since she had first arrived. She saw this as a promising sign.

Molly picked up the silver coffee pot and poured herself a cup. She looked across at her father with a quizzical smile. When he shook his head, she was surprised.

'No coffee?'

'Not for me.'

'Maybe half a cup?'

'No coffee, no tea, no beer, no spirits, no sex, no nothing. My assets are dwindling, Molly.'

'What do you do for kicks?'

'Look out at Central Park.'

He took a packet of cigarettes from the pocket of his cardigan and flicked one up expertly with his finger. As he slipped it between his lips, however, Molly gently removed it.

'I want a cigarette!' he protested.

'Resist the urge.'

'I don't want to.'

She read him the warning that was printed on the packet. '"The Surgeon General Has Determined That Cigarette Smoking Is Dangerous to Your Health" . . .'

'Screw the Surgeon General!'

She replaced the cigarette in the packet and then put it out of his reach. Sipping her coffee, she studied him with fond concern.

'How *do* you feel?'

'Old.'

'I thought it was just a flu.'

'The Bubonic Plague was just a flu.'

'What have they told you?'

'The usual load of nonsense.'

'And what was that?' she pressed.

'My heart is weak, my kidneys are failing, my lungs are

silting up, my waterworks are playing tricks, my brain is shrinking by the hour . . . Apart from that, I'm as good as new.'

'You need looking after,' she argued.

'That's why I employ Helen.'

'It's not the same.'

'Same as what?'

'I wish you'd come home with me.'

Disbelief tinged his voice. 'To *Ardsley*?'

'Pack your things and we'll go right now.'

'Christmas in the suburbs!'

'You make it sound like the North Pole.'

'It'd be worse. Far worse.'

'Give it a try.'

'No way!'

'Why not?'

'I'd spoil it.'

'No, you wouldn't.'

'Well, I'd sure as hell do my best.'

Molly sighed and leaned in closer to him.

'You're all the family I have. You should *be* there.'

'You should be *here*,' he retorted.

'I have a husband.'

'Oh yes. I keep forgetting.'

She bit back a reply and waited until she felt a little calmer. Then she sipped some more coffee before trying to reason with him.

'We'd love to have you. I'd love it and Brian would love it.'

'But I wouldn't.'

'Look, what have you got against Brian?' she asked.

'He's a doctor and I hate doctors.'

'Brian is your son-in-law!'

'That's his problem. All I know is that I am not spending Christmas in Ardsley so he can talk about my symptoms.'

23

'It won't *be* like that!' she promised.

There was an awkward silence that was only broken when Helen came in to clear the table. She was quick and efficient and they were soon left alone once more. Molly made a final attempt.

'Think about it.'

'I have.'

'If you change your mind, come on straight out.'

'Don't bank on it.'

She accepted defeat. 'OK. Play it your way.'

'I will.' He gave her a weary smile. 'And don't worry about me. I'll be alright. I'm such a pain in the ass these days. I deserve myself. Count yourself lucky I'm not coming.'

'I'll call you tomorrow.'

'I'll be here.'

'Merry Christmas . . .'

'What's merry about it?'

Molly left the apartment feeling sad and disappointed.

As a respite from shopping, Frank Raftis had called in at his office again and found that there was no hope of peace there. His secretary had a list of calls for him to make and other colleagues kept bursting in to discuss details of work in hand. He was beginning to think that shopping might be the easier option, after all.

'Oh, and Mr Rawlins called.'

'Vic? What did he want?'

'Nothing urgent. Some minor problems on site.'

Frank heard the alarm bell ring. 'There's no such thing as minor problems on this job!' he sighed. 'We only get the king-sized variety. Who'd be an architectural engineer?'

'I could always tell Mr Rawlins that you didn't come back to the office,' the girl suggested.

24

'Thanks, Leona. Better speak to him. Get him on the line.'

While his secretary made the telephone call, Frank spread some drawings out on his desk. His instincts were proved right. When Vic Rawlins came on the line, the minor problem had blown up into what was potentially a major setback. It took almost half an hour to sort it out. When Frank finally put down the receiver, he buried his face in his hands for a second.

'That is definitely that!' he announced, surfacing.

'No more calls?'

'I am not in, Leona.' He began collecting up his things. 'If anybody wants me, they'll have to wait till after Christmas.'

'Yes, Mr Raftis.'

'And I suggest that you call it a day pretty soon.'

'Thank you!'

'Oh, I almost forgot.' Frank burrowed among his presents and came up with a small package tied with a bow. 'Merry Christmas!'

'For me?' She was delighted.

'Not to be opened until tomorrow, Leona,' he warned. 'I hope you like it. Must dash . . .'

'Goodbye, Mr Raftis.'

'Bye . . .'

'And Merry Christmas!'

Leona lifted the package to her nose and sniffed it. Perfume. Her favourite. She smiled complacently and put the package in her bag.

Frank, by contrast, was inhaling the fumes of a hundred exhausts out in the street. Traffic was now thicker and slower and it was some time before an empty taxi crawled up to the kerb beside him. He dived into the back seat with his bags and parcels. The cab driver's tone was resentful.

'Where to, buddy?'

'Fifth Avenue.'

'Where?'

'Between 55th and 56th.'

'You're kidding!' exclaimed the other.

'No. Rizzoli's Bookstore.'

'You don't want to go there.'

'I do.'

'Well, you can't, buddy.'

'Why not?'

'Rush hour. You know? You ever hear of rush hour?'

'Yeah. I heard of rush hour.'

The driver rearranged Frank's plans for him. 'I'll take you downtown. Barnes and Nobles. It'll be faster.'

'I don't want faster. I want Rizzoli's.'

'Don't give me a hard time,' argued the driver. 'I get stuck in Fifth Avenue, I'll be there all day.'

Frank spotted a compromise solution. 'Alright, look. There's a side entrance on 56th street. You can leave me there.'

'Thanks a lot!' came the sarcastic reply.

It was a long, fraught, uncomfortable ride for both of them.

Molly Gilmore had the same trouble with her cab driver. Though he took her to her destination, he reserved the right to tell her that she would be wiser to go elsewhere to avoid the traffic. Since he was obviously feeling sorry for himself, she let him ramble on unchecked and simply threw in the occasional noise of assent. When he finally deposited her on the sidewalk, she gave him a large tip in order to get rid of him. Then she went into the building.

As Molly Gilmore entered Rizzoli's Bookstore through one door, Frank Raftis was pushing his way through another. Both of them were wishing that they had walked instead of taking a taxi.

They wandered through the rooms and galleries, hoping for inspiration. Each had come to buy another present for a marital partner and it was turning out to be a difficult assignment.

What could Molly buy for her husband? It was a question that had tormented her all her marriage and she had still not found the answer. Twice a year – at Christmas and on his birthday – she was in the same quandary. Brian had no hobbies to speak of and no real time for leisure. He was dedicated to his job and it seemed to absorb him completely. What do you buy a doctor? A new stethoscope? A set of syringes? Medical textbooks? Molly was on familiar territory. Searching for a non-existent present to be given to a man who would not appreciate or use it. And yet she did not give up. Convinced that if she stayed there long enough her question would at last be answered, she browsed her way through display after display.

Frank's problem was a carbon copy. How could he choose something that Ann would actually like? It was ironic. He could buy a gift for his secretary and be certain that Leona would love it, but when it came to his own wife, indecision set in like lockjaw. He was already having second thoughts about the negligee and wondering if he should go back and exchange it for the innocuous bath-robe. All those years of marriage to her and he was still dithering. Because she liked books, he had come to Rizzoli's but which one should he buy? He scanned the titles like a beachcomber living on hope.

Molly eventually found what she was after. It was called *The Big Book of Sailing* and was a superbly produced volume with colour and half-tone plates. Brian had once talked of taking up yachting. Admittedly, it had been a long time ago but the interest he expressed then was

27

enough to persuade Molly now that she had found the right present. She leafed through the pages with candid gratitude.

Gardening For All Seasons was Frank's salvation. A big, handsome, well-illustrated book, it reminded him that Ann was always saying that she would love to learn more about gardening. Here was something which she could enjoy reading and which would be of practical use. His confidence soared as he flicked through the book. Ann would love it. He was so pleased with his purchase that he even convinced himself that she would love the negligee as well.

Molly and Frank waited in parallel queues to be served. Cash registers were singing throughout the store. Last minute shopping was keeping the staff at full stretch. Queues slowly shortened.

'Thank you, sir.' The salesgirl took the book from Frank.

'I got nothing less,' he apologized, handing over a hundred dollar bill. 'Oh, and I'd like it wrapped.'

'Of course, sir . . .'

While the girl went about her work, he consulted his list for what he prayed would be the last time and saw that he had done very well. Almost all the items had been bought and the pencilled question marks after his wife's name could now be rubbed out. He had survived. He had run the gauntlet of another year's Christmas shopping and come through it relatively unscathed. He felt good.

'Here you are, sir . . .'

'Mm?' He was miles away.

'Your change.'

'Oh, thanks.'

'The book has been gift wrapped.'

'Great.'

Taking the money and thrusting it into his wallet, he

picked up his bags and headed quickly for the exit. He was pushing his way through the door when he was called back.

'Sir! Sir!' The girl had powerful lungs. 'Wait a minute!'

Frank stumbled back through the door. 'Me?'

'You forgot something.'

'I did?'

She held up the white carrier bag containing the book. In his eagerness to leave, he had omitted to pick it up. He went back to the counter, collected the purchase, shrugged an apology, then swung on his heel to go out again. But someone was now in his way, having come from the other cash register. The two of them collided. Frank was startled by the mild impact.

'What . . .?'

'Oh!'

'Sorry.'

'Sorry, I'm . . .'

'Here. Let me . . .'

Trying to get out of her way and open the door for her at the same time, he contrived to knock a couple of bags from her hand.

'Oh, Jesus!' he murmured.

'Wait . . .'

'Here . . .'

'It's OK.'

But it was not. As Frank bent down to retrieve her bags, he dropped some of his own, including the carrier bag containing the gardening book. His embarrassment brought colour to his cheeks.

'I was trying . . .'

'Let me help you . . .'

'. . . to do all this last-minute shopping . . .'

A man now came into the shop from behind him and the swinging door nudged yet another bag out of his hand.

Subdued panic brought the first hint of perspiration to his brow. Molly started to laugh. Frank was offended at first then he, too, saw the ridiculousness of the situation. They laughed quietly together and their mutual discomfort was eased at once.

Molly first bent to collect his bags and handed them to him one at the time, then she picked up her own things and got herself ready to depart. Both of them were now completely loaded with their Christmas shopping. It was at this moment that they looked at each other for the first time.

Some kind of recognition took place. Both of them were aware of it but their feelings were so confused that they could not analyze them. The closest they could get to it was to confess that they both experienced a fleeting interest in each other. Strangers becoming friends. A casual encounter taking on significance. Their paths had criss-crossed throughout the day without their even noticing. But here, in a crowded bookshop, at the end of a tiring Christmas Eve, they were at last seeing each other properly.

Frank cleared his throat and rose to a shy smile.

'Well . . .'

'Are you alright?'

'Yeah. Thanks. Yeah . . .'

He was about to say something else but it died on his lips.

'I must be . . . on my way,' she said.

'Me, too.'

'After you . . .'

'No, no,' he insisted, backing away from the door. 'After you . . .'

'Bye.' Molly went out briskly.

'Bye.'

He hesitated for a couple of seconds then followed her

out into Fifth Avenue. The sky was darkening now and the street lighting was on. Molly was heading south. Frank had a sudden impulse to go after her. Why? To do what? It was pointless. He controlled the impulse and turned in the opposite direction. What could he possibly have said to her? It was all over. He had somewhere else to go.

'Hey!' It sounded like her voice. 'Excuse me!'

'What?' He turned around.

Molly was running towards him. 'Hello . . .'

'Hello . . .'

'I'm sorry . . .'

'Why?'

'You . . . uh . . .'

She indicated the two white carrier bags in his right hand. Both had the name of the bookstore printed on them. In the confusion, he had evidently picked up her bag as well.

'Sorry . . .'

'My fault,' she conceded.

'No, mine.' He handed one of the bags to her. 'Here.'

'Thanks.'

Another look. Another feeling of recognition. More curiosity.

'Well . . .' Molly broke the spell. 'Merry Christmas.'

Frank beamed. 'Merry Christmas. Yeah. Merry Christmas.'

He watched her as she strolled away and again he felt the urge to follow her. It was up to him to take the initiative. How would she react? What possible harm could it do? Cathedral bells suddenly rang out to mark the hour and he was jerked forcibly out of his meditation. It was time to go home. After checking his watch, he forgot all about Molly Gilmore and hurried off in the other direction.

* * *

Brian was waiting for her at Ardsley Station and he took control immediately. Relieving her of her bags, he gave her a kiss on the cheek and lead her towards the car. Molly was glad to see him. She had been certain that he would be there. The first thing she had ever loved about Brian Gilmore was his reliability. His steadiness. She could count on him. It was an underrated virtue.

Even driving a car, he had a soothing bedside manner.

'Relax. You look dead beat.'

'It's been a long, long day . . .'

'Did you get everything you wanted?'

'More or less.'

'See Isabelle?'

'Briefly. She doesn't change!'

'And your father?' Out of the corner of his eye, he saw her purse her lips. 'So he's no better . . .'

'He's worse, Brian.'

'You know my diagnosis . . . Did you invite him?'

'Wouldn't hear of it. He thinks Ardsley is out in the sticks.'

'It is. That's its attraction . . .'

Molly kicked off her shoes and wriggled her toes. 'That's better!'

'You need a nice, restorative bath,' he prescribed.

'Yes, doctor . . .'

'I'll draw it for you.'

She touched his arm with distant affection.

Twenty minutes later, Molly was lying in hot, soapy water and starting to recover from the rigours of her day. She weighed her fatigue against her sense of achievement and decided that her outing had been a success.

Brian came into the bathroom with a warm drink for her. As she looked up at the tall, bearded figure of her husband, she noted yet again the kind eyes and the composed features. He was always on top of things. Calm and collected. In charge. It was inconceivable that a man like Brian Gilmore would drop his bags in a Manhattan bookstore, let alone walk off with someone else's purchase. He was a rock of dependability. Picking her up in the car. Drawing the bath. Making the drink. Loving her.

'Thanks, Brian . . .'

'I'll see you downstairs.'

'Won't be long . . .'

Judged against most husbands, Brian was a paragon. Molly had realized it a long time ago. But if this was so and if she was happily married to him, why were her thoughts turning once more to the stranger at Rizzoli's? She would never see the man again. Why did he keep coming back into her mind?

She reached for the drink and took a long sip.

The struggle of putting them both to bed told in her face. Ann looked as if she were half-asleep but there were still too many things to do before she could allow herself the luxury of turning in. Frank helped her to wrap the children's presents and place them under the Christmas tree. The living room was an amiable clutter and they both liked it that way. As they knelt side by side on the carpet in front of the fire, there was an easy togetherness about them that they had come to value deeply.

Ann wrapped the boxing gloves with great care.

'These could turn out to be a big mistake, Frank . . .'

'Every kid should learn how to take care of himself.'

'Mike and Joe fight enough as it is without being encouraged.'

'Take it from me, honey. They'll love the gloves.'

Her face was always improved by that warm smile. He leaned across to kiss her gently on the lips and smoothed the back of her dark, curly hair. He was about to kiss her again.

'We still have all these other presents to pack.'

'OK.' he accepted. 'First things first.'

'How was Manhattan?'

'Sheer chaos.'

'Have lunch with Ed?'

'Yeah. He's fine.'

'And Susan.'

'Oh . . . she's fine, too.'

Frank did not feel able to break the news of the divorce to her. Christmas was a time for happiness and for shared pleasures. It would be wrong to upset Ann now. Spoil the mood.

She yawned involuntarily. 'I'm tired.'

'That makes two of us. Much more to do?'

'Mountains.'

'I'll help . . .'

It was her turn to bestow a gentle kiss.

As he watched her arranging the presents carefully around the base of the tree, Frank was struck with what a good wife she really was. Ann was so easy-going and undemanding. Life with her brought no great strain – the children provided that! She did the important things well and she never let him down. Ann Raftis was something very special and he would tell her that later on.

Then he picked up the carrier bag from Rizzoli's bookstore and his wife flitted out of his mind as if she had never been there.

Chapter 3

Christmas morning began very early among the families of Westchester County. Children everywhere ignored the dire threats and impassioned pleas of their parents and responded instead to their own biological clocks. Hours before dawn lights were on in thousands of homes. It was a day of great expectations and the children were determined to enjoy it to the full.

Dobbs Ferry was like the rest of middle class suburbia. Groaning parents were roused from their slumbers and levered out of their beds. Many of them began to question the wisdom of having children, but most bowed to the inevitable with good grace and, after a third cup of coffee, actually began to share in the elation. It was the season of goodwill and it accommodated almost anything.

Joe Raftis came out of his sleep in an instant. His little fist banged on the table lamp and he threw back the sheets to run across to his elder brother. Mike felt the hand on his shoulder and came awake at once. The pair of them giggled with anticipatory delight. It was time to spread the good news that Christmas morning had arrived at last.

They raced along the landing to their parents' bedroom.

'I'm awake! I'm awake!'

'I was awake first!' insisted Joe.

'Merry Christmas! Merry Christmas!'

'Merry Christmas!'

If the deafening noise had not dragged Frank and Ann

from their sleep, then the physical pummelling would certainly have done the job. Using the bed as a trampoline, the two boys jumped and bounced until their father reached up to stop them.

'Hold on, fellas! Hold on!'

'It's Christmas Day!' announced Joe.

'Thanks for telling me . . .'

'Get up, Mommy!' urged Mike. 'Get up!'

'Stop leaping up and down like that!' she moaned.

'Give us time to wake up,' suggested Frank.

'Can we go downstairs?' asked Mike.

'And open the presents?' added Joe.

'You can go downstairs – and *wait*!' he told them.

'Aw!' they moaned in unison.

He ruffled their hair. 'Go on. Beat it.'

'Don't be long.'

'We'll be waiting.'

'Come on, Joe.'

'Race you . . .'

And the two of them sprinted out of the room together.

Ann pulled the coverlet up over her head. Frank nestled up to her and kissed her softly on the face. She murmured something.

'Merry Christmas,' he whispered.

'Please . . .'

'Don't you want to open your presents?'

'No . . .'

'Ann!'

'Whose idea was it to have children? Mine or yours?'

'Yours.'

'I must have been out of my mind.'

'Now you tell me!'

They laughed briefly then sat up in bed. He slipped an arm around her and began to kiss the back of her neck. Ann purred.

'We'd better go, Frank . . .'

'They can wait.'

'No.'

'What's the hurry?'

'Let's get it over with.'

She heaved herself out of bed, grabbed her robe and stalked out of the room. He sighed in disappointment. Then he remembered the boys and got out of bed himself.

Ten minutes later, he was sitting on the floor of the living room amid piles of discarded wrapping paper. Mike and Joe were thrilled with their presents and showed each one off as it was unwrapped.

'A baseball bat! My own baseball bat!'

'I got one, too!' shouted Joe.

'Will you play with us, Dad?'

'Will you take us outside?'

'Later.'

'Oh boy! I'll really give the ball a smack with this!'

'Don't swing it around like that, Mike,' advised his mother. 'You'll hit the tree.'

Mike dropped the bat and grabbed another present. While he tore off the paper, Ann was just finding the first of her gifts. She held up the negligee and laughed despite herself.

'Oh God!'

'What?' asked Frank, looking up.

'Well . . .'

'No good, huh?'

'It's beautiful.'

'You don't like it.'

'I do,' she said, uncertainly. 'It's . . . it's beautiful.'

'You can exchange it.'

'No, really. It's just . . . no, it's beautiful. It just surprised me, that's all. Really. It's so "romantic". Thank you.'

She gave him a token kiss and he wished that he had settled for the bathrobe. Ann was being polite about a present that she would probably never wear.

'Wow! Look at *these*!'

Mike had found his boxing gloves and was overjoyed. Joe was stricken with envy until he realized that he had been given a pair of his own. They pulled the gloves on at once then started to belabour their father.

'Take it easy! Take it easy!' he protested.

'They're great!' laughed Joe.

'Feel *this*!' warned Mike.

'You got a punch like Rocky Marciano,' complained Frank, pushing Mike away. 'Now back off, will you? I'll go three rounds with the pair of you later on. OK?'

'Can we fight each other?'

'No, Joe!' came the firm reply.

'Aw, Mom!'

'Take the gloves off and open the rest of your presents.'

'Yeah!' Mike approved of the idea.

Frank unwrapped one of his gifts from his wife and found a new shirt. It was useful but hardly exciting. He nodded his thanks to her but she was too absorbed in removing the paper from a book.

'What's this?' she asked.

'It's for your garden.'

'We're going to put a boat in the garden?'

'No, of course not.'

'Then why this?'

'Why what?'

'I don't get it.'

'Ann, it's not about boats.'

She handed him the book. 'You didn't buy a yacht, did you?'

Frank looked down at *The Big Book Of Sailing*. The

front cover showed a cluster of yachts out at sea. No sign of any garden.

'It *is* about boats,' he gulped.

'Would I lie to you?'

'I didn't buy this.'

'It's very nice.'

'But I didn't buy it, Ann.'

'I like books.'

'How in hell . . .'

She gave him another token kiss and went off towards the kitchen, throwing a general order over her shoulder.

'OK, everybody. Christmas is over. Let's clean up this mess.'

The boys did not hear her and Frank was still mesmerised by the book. He turned it over and shook his head in bafflement. Very slowly, he began to remember.

'Oh no . . .' He smiled. 'Oh no . . .' He laughed. 'Oh no . . .'

Realization visited Ardsley a few hours later. Holding a copy of *Gardening For All Seasons*, Molly Gilmore laughed to herself.

'Oh no . . . No! No!'

'It's a very nice book,' said Brian.

'Look, I'm sorry.'

'It is, Molly.'

'No, it's a mistake. There was a man in the store . . . I, uh, oh . . . never mind. Look, I'll take it back.'

'Well . . .'

'Really.'

She kissed him lightly on the cheek and tugged at the pullover he was wearing over his pyjamas in the vain hope that she could make it look better on him. Molly conceded defeat. The multicoloured pullover was ridiculous on Brian. He looked absurd and uncomfortable. She saw now that she should have bought him the cardigan. It would have suited his personality. Brian was Brian. A quiet, responsible, unsensational professional man. No garment could hide that fact.

'I'll take this back, too,' she offered.

'No, I like it. I told you. I do.'

'It's the wrong one for you, Brian.'

'I'll get used to it.'

'You'll never even wear it.'

He shrugged his assent. 'Anyway, it's the thought that counts.'

'That's what I mean. I'll take it back.'

Brian crossed to the table and poured her a glass of champagne. The living room at Ardsley was bigger than the one at Dobbs Ferry and it was more expensively decorated, but even with the Christmas tree and the decorations it had neat, ordered, meticulously clean air about it that made it seem almost hollow. The house in Dobbs Ferry was a typical family home: this one was decidedly less lived in. It reflected Brian's tastes for the most part and he preferred a large, comfortable, hygienic environment.

'Here's yours,' he said, handing her a glass.

'Thanks.' She raised it. 'Merry Christmas.'

'Yeah.'

She drank some champagne. 'Perfect!'

'Very acceptable,' he agreed, tasting it.

'Leave the bottle within reach.'

'We'd better get dressed, Molly.'

'Why?'

'Irene and Phil.'

'Oh no!'

'Oh yes . . .'

'When?'

'Brunch.'

40

'And when did *this* happen?' she complained.

'Come on,' he coaxed. 'It'll be fun.'

'Brian, it's Christmas morning.'

'Look, we don't have to go if you don't want to.' He gestured to the sofa. 'We can sit here all day and sing Christmas carols if you want to. It's up to you.'

Molly walked across the room and gazed out through the front window. The road was deserted. There were lights in the neighbouring houses. Distant laughter filtered through from someone's garden. Children's voices piped.

Brian came up behind her and put his arms around her.

'I thought we could just spend the day together,' she said.

'We *will* be together.'

'Together with Irene and Phil!'

'Get dressed, he advised, squeezing her shoulders. 'I'm going into town, get some gas.'

Brian went off upstairs and she was left to finish her drink alone. She looked up at the tall Christmas tree so full of bright promise, then down at the presents that lay opened on the floor. Irene and Phil. Effectively, her Christmas would be over.

She picked up the telephone and dialled a number.

'Yeah?' Her father sounded gruff and unsociable.

'Welcome to the day!'

'I'm still in bed.'

'Have you opened my present yet?'

'What present?'

'The one I left with Helen yesterday. You know quite well what present!' she scolded. 'Stop being difficult.'

'It's my trademark.'

She smiled. 'How are you today?'

'Ask me when I've opened my eyes properly.'

'Got something nice lined up?'

'She's stripping off in the next room.'

Molly laughed. 'And how are you *really* going to spend Christmas Day?' she wondered.

'Watching television.'

'You should have come to us.'

'I got a television of my own.'

'Alright, have it your way,' she sighed.

'Can I go back to sleep now?'

'Merry Christmas. Oh, and Brian sends his love.'

'Who the hell's Brian?'

'My husband. Now don't play games!'

'Oh yes. The doctor. Why do I always forget him?'

He hung up and Molly put down the receiver at her end. The thought of her father sitting alone in his huge apartment saddened her. Yet would he really have a better time with them? He and Brian under the same roof? She forced to act as referee? Maybe it was better the way it was. The line of least resistance.

She poured herself more champagne and the telephone rang.

'Hello?'

'Molly?' said a familiar husky voice. 'Irene here . . .'

'Irene!' She did her best to sound pleased.

'Merry Christmas, darling!'

'Same to you.'

'Did Brian tell you?'

'Yes. It'll be fine.'

'Are you sure? We'd hate to break up any plans . . .'

'We'd love to come,' lied Molly, convincingly. 'What time?'

'Eleven. Can't wait to show you what Phil's given me.'

'We'll be there.'

'Nice, quiet Christmas celebration with friends,' promised Irene. 'Just the four of us . . . Though Jack and Velma will join us later.'

'Oh.'

'And Jerry Danziger said he might drop in as well.'

'I see.'

'Don't be late, darling.'

'No.'

'Bye . . .'

Molly replaced the receiver again and glanced ruefully up at the ceiling. Brian had let them in for a fairly gruesome morning. However it turned out, it would not be her idea of Christmas. She emptied her glass quickly and filled it once more.

The New Year brought snow to Westchester County and sledges were out in abundance on the hillsides. Travellers were inconvenienced but the children were delighted, especially as the white carpet seemed to remain for much longer than usual. Snowmen popped up everywhere and frozen ponds tempted ice skaters. Roads had to be cleared then gritted. Plumbers were in demand throughout the county as pipes burst or drains became blocked.

Snow redefined the magic of the landscape and created some stunning new vistas but they still failed to capture the attention of the commuters who sped past them. It seemed as if nothing that Nature could do would make people stand and stare.

February maintained and even tightened the icy grip and it was not until well into March that temperatures started to rise. Flowers at last appeared in gardens and trees and shrubs put forth some hints of blossom. The winter was over. Spring gathered momentum and supplied all its traditional virtues. Birdsong was much more confident and much less plaintive.

Travel was now vastly easier for the majority of people. Frank Raftis was one of the few exceptions to the rule. He wondered why.

'Is it the alternator again?'

'Nope.'

'The battery?'

'Nope.'

'It must be something. Just went dead on me.'

The mechanic raised his head from under the hood. 'You got problems, Mr Raftis. The starter motor. Shorted the whole system.'

'That's all I need!'

'I'll have to tow it to the garage.'

'Any chance of a lift to the station on the way?'

'Climb aboard.'

'This car is jinxed,' decided Frank, getting into the passenger seat of the tow-truck. 'It breaks down as soon as you look at it.'

'Some cars are like that, Mr Raftis.'

The mechanic lowered the hood on Frank's Oldsmobile then winched the vehicle up so that only its rear wheels stayed in contact with the ground. He clambered into the driving seat and gunned the motor.

'What time's your train?'

'We should make it.'

'I'll go the quick way.' He embarked on an elaborate short-cut and dipped into his memoirs as they drove along. 'You think you got problems with that machine? Lemme tell you something. I once bought this Chevvy from a dealer in the Bronx. Mechanically – it was just beautiful. Went like a dream. The chassis – not bad! But that old Chevvy had one little problem. Ask me what it was.'

'What was it?' obliged Frank.

'Mice.'

'Mice?'

'Yeah – mice. You ever heard of a car with mice before? Well, that's what this one had. In the upholstery. You could hear them scratching. I tried everything. Traps.

Poison. Knives. Screwdrivers. Even rode around for a week with a cat on the back seat. But could I catch them? No sir! They were as much a part of that goddam Chevvy as the wheels. In the end, I learned to live with it. I ask you, Mr Raftis, what else *could* I do?'

Frank smiled. Mice in the upholstery. It was a good story. He wondered how many times the mechanic had told it. Against all the odds, Frank began to enjoy his journey to the station.

The same could not be said for Molly Gilmore. As she was driven to Ardsley Station by her husband, she sat brooding quietly. Her face was puckered and her hands were bunched tightly. Brian glanced across at her and saw how tense she seemed.

'I can pick you up if you take the 6:25.'

'Great.'

'Are you alright?'

'What? Yes. What?'

'All this. Back and forth.'

'I know. I'm alright, Brian. I'm just tired.'

'Who wouldn't be?' he consoled.

'No. It's not just him. He's no trouble, really. He's so frail now. He's not the problem.'

'Then what is?'

'Me. I think. No energy. No . . . I don't know.'

He reached across for her hand and kissed it gently. They drove on for a couple of blocks before he spoke again.

'Did you order the wine for Saturday?'

'What?'

'Saturday. the dinner party.'

'Oh god . . .'

'Oh no.'

'I'm sorry, I really am, Brian.'

45

'But I asked you *weeks* ago, Molly.'

'Went clean out of my mind . . .'

'Won't have anything left . . .'

'I'm very, very sorry . . .'

'. . . get stuck with some weird Roumanian chablis . . .'

'I'll call them.'

'Never mind, I'll do it.'

'No, leave it to me,' she offered.

'I did. This time, *I'll* handle it. You have enough to think about.'

'That's true . . .'

Nothing more was said until they reached the station. Molly got out of the car and came around to the driver's side. Brian lowered his window and leaned his head out.

'Take care of yourself, will you, please?'

'I'll try,' she promised.

'Good.'

There was a pause. 'I wish you would come and visit him.'

He kissed her on the cheek to avoid answering.

'I'll see you tonight.'

Molly watched him as he drove away. She had never understood the antipathy between her husband and her father. How could two people whom she loved so much hate each other like that? There had been trouble from the start. Her father had never approved of Brian as a potential husband and the friction had been constant. Since meetings between the two men always led to argument or embarrassment, they had elected to stay apart as much as possible. The rift widened imperceptibly. Pride was at stake on both sides. Neither man was ready to make the effort to see the other.

To all intents and purposes, they were enemies. What pained Molly Gilmore the most was that feeling that she was somehow to blame for the situation. Moving between the two men, she ended up giving only a part of herself to each. Both of them resented this and demanded more of her attention. Molly became both the symptom and the victim of the relationship between the two men.

The thunder of the approaching train directed her to her immediate priority. She ran into the station, bought a ticket and trotted out on to the platform. Doors slid open to welcome her.

The journey gave her an opportunity to muse even further on the strange life she was now living, shuttling to and from Manhattan each day, dividing her time between a sick father and a preoccupied husband. Little wonder that she was exhausted. Apart from the travelling, there was the continual effort of apologizing to one man on behalf of the other and groping blindly for some sort of reconciliation between them. Molly no longer had a firm anchorage. In a job, in a marriage, in a family. She had temporarily abandoned her career. She had found her role as a doctor's wife unfulfilling. And her relationship with her father had somehow worsened as he became more and more unwell.

She had slipped her emotional moorings and was adrift.

The slowing of the train brought her back to reality. They were coming into Dobbs Ferry Station and she spared it a half-glance. Standing on the platform was a tall man with close-cropped black hair that was slicked neatly back. His face had a hazy familiarity but she could not place him. Maybe he reminded her of someone else. Or maybe she noticed him because he was attractive. Molly did not know and in any case it was not important.

She was soon deep in thought once again.

Frank Raftis walked down the aisle until he found a seat. He took out his newspaper and started to scan the headlines. To his right and one seat in front of him was a woman with long auburn hair. He paid her no heed as he read about a speech on Defence given by President Reagan. Frank was still wading through the rhetoric when the conductor came into the car at the far end.

'Tickets, please! Tickets, please!'

He put his hand into his pocket to get his ticket at exactly the moment that Molly turned her head to see where the conductor was. Frank saw her and their eyes locked for a few moments. Each had a glimmer of recognition but it was certainly no more. They smiled out of embarrassment, looked away, looked back again, then turned away once more. The conductor moved up the aisle between them and prevented further eye contact.

'Tickets, please! . . . Thank you, sir . . .'

'Here . . .'

'Thank you . . . Have your tickets ready, please!'

Frank studied the auburn hair that was being worn shoulder-length. Where had he seen her before? Why had she seem to know him? Who was she? In the battle for his attention, President Reagan was fighting a losing battle on Defence. Though Frank pretended to skim through the article, his mind was still sifting through a series of possibilities. Was she someone he had met at a party?

Molly was asking herself the same questions about him. Then she caught herself doing it and felt that it was wrong of her. The man was a stranger. It was wrong of her to construct fantasies about him. She had noticed him because he was there. No other reason. Her mind should be on her father not on anyone else. Least of all on a chance meeting with a man who happened to think that he knew her.

The train powered on, its wheels clicking rhythmically on the tracks like so many metallic heartbeats. Molly listened to them and was almost lulled off to sleep. Frank heard them, too, and idly began to count them. Manhattan was getting nearer all the time.

When the train hurtled into the tunnel, the noise was

almost ear-splitting. It came out into Grand Central Station and slowed to a grinding halt. Regular commuters were on the move at once, going through yet another part of a sacred morning ritual, elbowing for position in the crowd on the platform. Frank was still gathering his things together as people pushed past him. Molly, too, seemed to be taking her time. She stepped into the aisle just behind him and they moved towards the exit.

Both were aware of how close they were to each other. Frank suddenly spun round to face her.

'Rizzoli's!' he exclaimed, pointing a finger at her.

'What?'

'Rizzoli's. Rizzoli's Bookstore.'

Molly was bewildered. 'I'm sorry . . .'

'I was trying to recall where . . .'

'. . . don't understand what . . .'

'. . . came to me in a flash. Rizzoli's!'

'Oh my god . . .' She had remembered as well.

'The books.'

'Yes.'

'I was . . .'

'I know, I know.'

Now she was pointing at him. They laughed happily together.

'I kept looking at you,' he explained. 'I knew I knew you from somewhere but I didn't know where.'

'You had all those packages.'

'I took yours.'

'My book on sailing. I had yours.'

'My book on gardening.'

'What did you do?'

'Took it back to Rizzoli's and exchanged it. You?'

'The same.'

'Yeah . . .'

'Well . . .'

He was grinning now and very pleased with himself.

'Anyway, I remembered.'

She hesitated. 'I'm . . . uh, well, I'm *glad* you remembered.'

'Thanks . . .'

A long, uneasy silence followed. Both of them felt an attraction but neither of them knew what to do about it beyond standing there with a forced smile. It was Molly who finally took the initiative.

'So,' she said, offering her hand. 'It's good to see you again.'

'Yes . . . I mean, it's good to see you, too.'

He shook her hand and held on to it slightly too long.

Another awkward pause. Molly eventually shrugged.

'I'd better . . .'

'Oh sure. Well. Merry Christmas'

'What?' She laughed. 'Oh yes. Merry Christmas.'

They went out on to the platform and nodded a farewell to each other. Molly walked on ahead and he kept his eyes on her. She turned back for an instant and he collected another smile from her. It made his grin widen at once.

Molly was now moving with a spring in her step. When she got on to the train, she felt tired and lethargic: when she left it, she was full of energy and bounce. For the first time in months, she was feeling terrific.

And she had no idea why.

Chapter 4

Hospitals were in league with death. The longer you stayed in one, the less likely you were to come out alive. Instead of making you better, a hospital had a vested interest in making you worse. The nursing staff was in on the conspiracy. So were the doctors. None of them would ever *tell* you anything. It was deliberate. All part of the insidious process of breaking you down. They cut you off from the outside world so that they could disorientate you. They put you on drip-feeds so that they could trap you. They subjected you to surgery so that they could maim and weaken you. A hospital was a euphemism for legalized murder. The crowning irony was that it made you pay for its treatment. You were actually subsidizing your own demise.

Such were the fevered thoughts that raced through the mind of John Trainer as he lay half-asleep in a private room at the hospital. His illness had taken its toll on him. The eyes were hollowed, the cheeks sunken and the flesh speckled. He looked five years older than he had done on Christmas Eve. Needing someone to blame, he fixed on the medical profession. The hospital staff coped very well with him and tolerated all his outbursts.

A nurse came into the room with something on a tray.

'I've brought you a drink, Mr Trainer.'

'Arsenic or strychnine?'

'Now don't start all that again . . .'

'I won't touch it,' he said with feeble authority.

'But you sent for it, Mr Trainer. Freshly-squeezed orange.'

'Orange . . .?'

'*I'll* see that he drinks it, Nurse.'

Molly was standing in the doorway holding a bunch of flowers. The nurse put the drink on the bedside cabinet then crossed over to her.

'Thank you, Mrs Gilmore.'

'How is he today?'

'Comfortable.'

'Does he doze off much?'

'All the time . . .'

The nurse went out and Molly looked over at her father. His eyes had closed and his breathing was a shade heavier. She tiptoed across to the bed and peered at him more closely. His eyelids began to flicker. Molly bent over him.

'Hi. Are you awake?'

He tried to focus on her. 'Molly?'

'Hi.'

'It's you.'

'What?'

'I'm still asleep.'

'I'll go away, then.'

'No, don't.'

'Feeling tired?'

'Give me time . . .'

She showed him the flowers. 'Brought you these.'

'Ah.' His hand fluttered. 'There's a . . . there's a . . .'

'I know where the vase is,' she said, moving to the table that stood in the window. She lifted a bunch of flowers from the vase and put them in the bin, then she started to arrange the freshly cut flowers. She sniffed them to savour their scent. 'I'll ask the nurse to put clean water in here.'

'Your mother used to bring home flowers every other day. She said they made her happy.'

'I don't remember her that way.'

'What way?'

'Happy. I remember the fights. I remember the days I was afraid to come into the house. But I don't remember happy.'

He thought it over. 'No. We were never happy.'

'Why not?'

'We were too much in love.'

'You were? Really? Do you mean that?'

'Oh, yes. For thirty years. It nearly killed me.'

'You were lucky,' observed Molly.

'We were miserable.'

'It doesn't sound so bad.'

'Well, that was another time,' he reflected with a sigh. 'The world was a very different place then. People don't fall in love any more. They're too busy trying to be happy.'

She was struck by the remark and thought about it for some time. When she looked back at him, he was indicating his throat.

'Dry?' He nodded and she reached for the glass of orange. She lifted his head with one hand and held the drink to his lips. 'Take it nice and easy . . . That's it . . .'

'Thanks . . .'

'Any time.'

'When are you going to get married, Molly?'

'What?'

'Your mother and me always hoped that one day you'd . . .'

'I *am* married,' she affirmed.

'Oh? Nobody told me.'

'Cut the wisecracks, buster,' she said good-humouredly. 'You *know* I'm married. You were at the wedding.'

'That's right. So I was. His name is Burt.'

'Brian.'

'I was near enough.' He pondered for a time then jabbed a finger at her. 'He's an orderly!'

'A doctor.'

'Well, he sure looked like an orderly to me.'

'Brian is a very successful doctor.'

'Kills lots of patients, you mean?'

'Stop it!' she told him, a smile tugging at her lips.

'Does he make you happy?'

'He tries to.'

'And? Anything to show for it?'

Molly nodded her head. 'Yes. I think he makes me happy . . .'

'So you're not in love with him.'

'Look, what is this . . .?'

'He didn't look the loving type to me. Orderlies never are.'

'He's a doctor!'

'Funny thing. I never found a doctor I could trust . . .'

The effort of making conversation had taxed him. His eyes filmed over and his head dropped back. Molly kissed him on the forehead and adjusted the pillow to make him more comfortable. She stayed there for some time looking down at him and remembering her childhood. He had been a kind but not indulgent father. As a husband, however, he had had many failings. When Molly thought about her mother she recalled a thin, pale woman who always seemed to be on the verge of tears. Mrs Gilmore could be argumentative and frequently yelled at her husband, but Molly's impression was that her mother had come off worse in marital combat.

Her own marriage was completely different. Molly and Brian had never had the kind of violent rows that were normal behaviour in her parents' house. They had disagreements, of course, but Brian almost never raised his voice. He hated to lose control and could somehow keep his cool in the most trying circumstances. It was a quality that Molly had always admired in him but it did make her feel thwarted sometimes. Deprived of a row that might have cleared the air. Denied the chance to let off steam.

Was she happy with Brian? It was something she never really thought about. She was fairly contented with her lot, certainly, and she always looked forward to seeing him. But was that happiness or simply force of habit?

Molly reversed the question. Was Brian happy with her? He seemed to be. She did her best to run the home the way that he liked it and she let him make the running in their social life. Most men would be happy in his shoes. But Brian was not like most men. He was not the happy type. Quiet satisfaction was more his style.

Were they in love?

It was the one question she could answer.

The huge empty shell of the building stared with sightless eyes at the East River. Men crawled all over it, giant cranes hoisted steel girders, dust-covered trucks spewed out their ready-mixed concrete, the makeshift elevator was in constant use. Winter snow had delayed work on the construction site and everyone was trying to make up for lost time. There was a clamour and urgency about all the activity. The men were on good wages and there were contract deadlines to be met. Everyone pitched in.

'Frank! Frank, did you hear me?'

'What . . .?'

'I was saying something important.'

'Yeah . . .'

Frank Raftis was rising in the elevator with Vic Rawlins, the architect of the building. Both men wore hard hats and both had to shout above the clatter all around them. The elevator stopped at the seventh floor and they stepped out on to bare concrete.

'Houston! Houston!' Vic almost bellowed. 'We were talking about Houston, Frank.'

'Texas.'

'Right. Where the hell *are* you?'

'I don't know. I was thinking about somebody.'

'Well, think about Houston, will you? Nine months, Frank. Ten at the outside.'

'A year, at *least*.'

'No way. It's the same design.'

Frank shook his head. 'I can't, Vic. I have family. You can find somebody out there.'

'I *have* somebody out there. I want you to consult. That's all.'

'If I consult, it's not my building.'

'So?'

'No deal.'

'Listen, I'm the architect. I'm supposed to be the prima donna. Not you. You're just the engineer.'

The transmitter beeped in Frank's top pocket. He unhooked it, threw a switch and spoke into the machine.

'Raftis . . .'

'Hi, Frank. Where are you?'

'Up on the seventh floor.'

'Can you spare me some time later on?' asked the voice.

'Sure, Louis. Catch me after lunch.'

'Thanks . . .'

The transmitter crackled and Frank replaced it in his pocket. When he looked across at Vic Rawlins, his colleague was clearly still waiting for a decision. Frank rubbed his chin.

'Let me think about it,' he said.

'Say yes. You can think about it later.'

'I don't know, Vic. I mean . . . Houston!'

'What's wrong with Houston!'

'Houston is not New York, that's what's wrong with Houston.'

'You're an engineer,' reminded Vic. 'You got to travel.'

'Well . . .'

'Nine months, Frank. At most.'

'What do I do with my house?'

'Rent it out while you're away. Sell it. Burn it down. Who cares what you do with it? I want you in Houston.'

'Leave it with me, Vic . . .'

'It's a big opportunity. Don't miss it.'

'Need to discuss it with Ann.'

'She'd love Houston. I know it.'

'We got a lot of things to keep us here,' warned Frank. 'So don't go building up your hopes, will you?'

Vic slapped him on the back. 'You won't let me down! Besides, a change would do you good. Manhattan is a jungle. Now, Texas . . . Texas is something different again.'

'Remember what General Sheridan said about Texas?'

'What?'

'He said that if he owned Hell and Texas, he'd live in Hell and rent out Texas. Maybe there's something in that.'

'Frank . . .'

'Come on. We got work to do.'

They went on a tour of inspection and checked everything in detail. As they moved around the building, Vic tried to pressurize Frank into committing himself but the latter was pleasantly evasive. By the time they had finished, it was the end of a long morning.

'Why don't I buy you lunch?' offered Vic. 'We could have a proper chat about the Houston deal.'

'We've *had* a proper chat.'

'But we didn't talk money.'

'No point, Vic. Besides, my lunch hour is already booked up. I'm playing tennis.' He raised a hand as Vic was about to speak. 'Don't rush me. I promised I'll think it over.'

'Good and hard.'

'Sure.'

They shook hands and parted. Frank dismissed the proposition from his mind and hurried off to find a cab. He was due to play Ed Lasky at the Manhattan Plaza Racquet Club. He was in the mood for some strenuous exercise and felt sure that he could give his opponent a tough time.

'Stop! Stop!' Ed Lasky agreed with him.

'Let's finish the game at least.'

'Enough! Enough!' gasped the other, leaning on the net for support. 'What's got into you, Frank? I expected a nice, gentle game of tennis – not three sets with John McEnroe!'

'I'm on song today, that's all.'

'You can say that again!'

They were playing on one of the many courts under the great glass bubble and other games continued all around them. Rubber squealed underfoot, racquets whistled through the air and the thwack of strings against tennis balls reverberated loudly. It was rather like being in an echo chamber.

Ed slumped down on the bench at the side of the court and mopped at his face with a towel. He was breathing stertorously and the sweat was streaming out of him. Frank sat beside him with his own towel around his neck.

'What's the matter, Ed?'

'I'm having a heart attack.'

'You deserve a heart attack. What have you been doing to yourself?'

'Worst weekend of my entire life.'

'What happened?'

Ed emerged from the towel and rolled his eyes in mock agony.

'Everything. Carol and I were supposed to go away for

the weekend. Friday, my wife calls. Can I take the kids on Saturday and Sunday? She's not feeling well. So we cancel the weekend, the kids are with us, we go to a movie, and guess what?'

'Tell me.'

'We run into my wife. She's with some man. Some real finky-looking guy. I get pissed off, my wife is embarrassed, the kids are confused, Carol hits the ceiling and throws me out. Saturday night, eleven o'clock, I'm on the street with two kids, three suitcases and a dog.' He paused for effect. 'She wants to get married.'

'The dog?'

'Carol! Carol wants to get married.'

'You're not divorced yet.'

'I know, I know . . . Hey, look at *that*!'

'Where?'

'Right there . . .'

Frank glanced in the direction indicated by his friend. On the adjoining court, an attractive, long-legged blonde was starting to knock up with her partner. Ed positively growled with delight.

'Who *is* that? Do we know her?'

'Uh, no. I don't.'

'Strong legs,' noted Ed. 'I was seeing somebody once, had legs like that. Every time I went down on her, I dislocated my neck. How do *you* do it?'

'Do what?'

'With Ann.'

'Oh . . .'

'Yeah.'

'Well . . .' Frank hunched his shoulders.

Ed became philosophical. 'Some men are smarter. About cheating. Like you. You're smarter.'

'Let's play some more tennis.'

'See? Smart.'

59

'I was serving. Forty-love.'

They moved back to the court but Frank was no longer thinking about the game. He was back on the morning train into Grand Central Station. He was still chuckling to himself as he served.

The restaurant was crowded and they had to wait for their lunch but neither of them minded. They were enjoying their conversation so much that time meant nothing to them. Isabelle blinked in astonishment.

'Love? Are you kidding?'

'No. Really. He said they were in love for thirty years.'

'Please, Molly! Don't start with love.'

'What? Why?'

'Because I'm not interested,' asserted Isabelle, pouring some more wine into her glass. 'I've done my time with love. I just want to have fun now. You know?'

'You're lying,' decided Molly.

'I'm not lying. I don't believe in it. I mean, really, anybody who falls in love these days deserves everything he gets. Or *she* gets, as the case may be.'

'But all those men . . .'

Isabelle cackled with pleasure. 'Yes. All those men!'

'What's the point?'

'I'm telling you, the point is have some fun. What do you think *they're* after? Love? Hearts and flowers? Give me a break!'

Molly tried to fight off disillusion. 'Well . . .'

'Well what?'

'Well, there *has* to be something else.'

'Yeah. Fantasy. Dreams. All those fairy tales we grew up with. Bullshit! There *is* no white knight. Believe me!' She sipped her drink. 'I'll tell you something else, too. All those fairy tales were written by men.'

'But something does "happen" between two people. Doesn't it?'

'Sure. Sex.'

Molly laughed. 'I give up, Isabelle. You just don't *want* to believe in it.'

'No, I don't,' agreed the other. 'Fancy a dessert?'

'Why not?' She pushed the menu away as Isabelle offered it to her. 'I don't want anything . . . You said you don't believe in love. Why not? Go on, tell me. Why not?'

'Because it's too painful. Ah, God. Look. Have an affair, will you? Get it out of your system.'

'What?' Molly almost blushed.

'That's what we're talking about, isn't it?'

'No. No.' A thoughtful pause. 'No.'

Isabelle smiled knowingly and leaned across the table to take hold of her wrist. The voice was low and conspiratorial.

'I'll make a bargain with you. *I* choose the dessert for both of us and *you* tell me all about him.'

'But there's nothing to tell . . .'

Nevertheless, Molly told it for the next half an hour. Isabelle listened with interest and made sage comments from time to time. She was delighted to see some human fallibility in her friend, and she noted how animated Molly was while talking.

At length they left the restaurant and came out into the street. Isabelle pressed for more detail. Molly kept shrugging compulsively.

'I don't know . . . nice. Sort of . . . yeah, nice . . . I don't know. He looked . . . He looked familiar.'

'And that's it? That's the whole story? You met in Rizzoli's on Christmas Eve and then met him again today on the train?'

'Yes. Except . . .'

'Go on.'

'Except that for a minute, I thought . . . it was nothing. It was just. I don't know. Something.'

'Sure. What's his name? I probably know him.'

'His name?'

'Doesn't he have a name?'

'Of course he does, Isabelle.'

'So what is it? Don't be bashful.'

'I don't *know* his name.'

'Didn't you *ask*?'

'No.'

'But you told him your name, surely?'

'No.'

Isabelle was aghast. 'What in hell's name are you two playing at? There are rules, you know. Little niceties. You want to go to bed with someone, you at least find out their name first.'

'It isn't *like* that!' protested Molly.

'It's always like that, honey.'

'You make everything about sex.'

'I do my best.'

'It was just . . . a funny coincidence.'

'Yeah. You want him and he wants you . . .'

'No, Isabelle! It was only . . . coincidence.'

They walked to the end of the block then waited for the lights to change. Isabelle turned and looked her full in the eyes.

'O.K. Coincidence. I buy that. Still leaves the big question.'

'Question?'

'What are you going to do about it?'

Molly laughed. 'Oh you! You're incorrigible!'

The sauna was like a small furnace and both men were sweating freely. Ed Lasky sat naked on the lower bench with his hands on his knees while Frank Raftis was stretched out on the upper level where the heat was more punitive. Naked but for the wet towel over his face, Frank was trying to fend off his friend's interrogation.

'Drop it, will you, Ed?'

'Aw, come on!'

'I'm telling you – no.'

'You *never* had an affair?' asked the other in tones of incredulity. 'Never ever?'

'No.'

'Not even a quickie?'

'No.'

'Not even a normal, healthy one-night stand?'

'You don't believe me, do you?'

'What do you take me for, Frank? Of course, I don't believe you.'

'Nobody believes me. That's why I never say it.'

Ed ruminated. 'That's really disgusting. I mean, all these years I've known you . . . That's really disgusting.'

Frank smiled under the wet towel then sat up.

'I met a woman on the train this morning.'

'Yeah?' Interest quickened. 'And? And?'

'Nothing.'

Ed became morose. 'I don't want to get married again.' He considered the problem. 'But I don't like being alone.' He ran a forearm across his face to remove some of the sweat. 'What did she look like?'

'Who?'

'The woman on the train.'

'Nice. She looked . . . nice.'

'What kind of nice? Nice to talk to? Nice to be with? Nice in bed? There's nice and nice.'

'I need a cold shower . . .'

Ed chuckled. 'Oh *that* kind of nice!'

'No. I'm baking in here, that's all. Had enough.'

'Me, too. So don't think you're escaping. We'll carry this discussion further . . .'

'There's nothing to discuss, Ed.'

'Don't give me that. I got a nose for these things. You're hiding something, Frank, and I'm going to find out what it is.'

They had a cold shower then Frank immersed himself in the ice-cold plunge bath. Ed kept up his cross-questioning throughout and did not even relent when the two men were having a friction rub from the attendants. Frank slowly told him the salient details. The meeting at Rizzoli's. Wrong books. Seeing her on the train that morning. Simply enjoying the woman's company.

As they dressed in the locker room, Ed continued to probe.

'So what was her name?'

'Name?'

'Yeah. Her name. She has a name, doesn't she?'

'Sure.'

'Well?'

'I didn't ask her.'

'You're incompetent!'

'Ed, I wasn't trying to pick her up.'

'Why not?'

'I'm married, that's why not. And I've never . . .'

'Never picked a woman up in your life. Yeah, I know!'

'It's true.'

'Why don't you level with me, Frank?'

'I have. It's just a funny story, that's all. I'm sorry I mentioned it. Forget it.'

They finished dressing in silence, packed up their things and came out of the club into warm sunshine. Ed resumed his questioning.

'When are you going to see her again?'

'How do I know?'

'You didn't even make a date?' Ed sounded appalled.

'Of course not.'

'I thought you liked the woman.'

'Ed . . .'

'Did you or didn't you? Why be coy about it?'

'OK. I liked her.'

'Enough to want to see her again?'

'Maybe.'

'So what are you going to do about it?'

'Look, will you get off my back?'

'I'm serious.'

'What am I supposed to do?' asked Frank with irritation. 'Hang around Grand Central until she shows up? Give her some line? Take her to a hotel? What are you talking about?'

'Well . . .'

'It was just a thing that happened, Ed. That's all. I don't know what it was. It was nice. That's all. That's all there was to it.'

Ed Lasky smirked. He knew better.

It was not really out of her way. By walking three extra blocks, she was able to turn into the store and pretend that she had been passing it in any case. Also, she did have a legitimate reason for being there. Irene had been so complimentary about a new cookery book that Phil had given her for her birthday. Molly had always meant to find the book and make her own judgement. This would be a good opportunity. By the time she reached the cookery section, she had convinced herself that she had a desperate need to come to Rizzoli's Bookstore. It was pure chance that it had also been the venue of her first meeting with the stranger on the train.

The place was relatively empty that afternoon with just a few people browsing here and there. Molly checked out the cookery book but decided against buying it. Apart from the expense, it featured far too many calorific dishes and Brian was very much into health foods. She wandered amiably through the various departments and examined the occasional book to show willing. Then she came to the section where she had been on Christmas Eve and crossed to the display table. *The Big Book of Sailing* was no longer there but *Gardening For All Seasons* had pride of place.

Seeing it sent a tiny thrill throughout her body.

She picked up the book and she heard his voice again.

'Can I help you?'

'What?' She turned to see the sales assistant beside her.

'Did you want that book?'

'Uh, no. No, thanks . . . I was only . . . uh, no.'

She replaced the volume and smiled an apology at the assistant. Then she went through the door and out into the street, wondering why she had behaved like that and how it was that she felt so guilty.

At the same time, she was glad that she had visited Rizzoli's again. It had been well worth the additional walk.

Chapter 5

Ann Raftis picked the children up as usual in her car and drove them straight back to the house. A long day at school had not diminished their energy in any way. They were keen for more action.

'Take us to the park, Mom.'

'Not now, Mike.'

'But we got to practice.'

'Dad's going to play baseball with us this weekend,' added his younger brother. 'Boy, wait till he sees me pitch!'

'Come on, Mom. Take us.'

'Go in the garden.'

'It's not the same,' argued Mike.

Joe was quick to support his brother. 'No. You hit a homer out there and you break someone's window.'

'Why can't we go to the park?'

'Because I've got too many things to do . . .'

The argument continued for another five minutes until Ann threatened to confiscate the baseball bats altogether. Nursing rebellion, the boys agreed to go out into the garden. Ann finished some of her household chores then started in on a number of telephone calls that she had to make. Last on the list was her husband.

'Hi there!'

'Hello . . .'

'How's it all going?' she asked.

'I've had quieter days.'

'So have I. What's the position with the car?'

'Not good, Ann.'

'Oh . . .'

'I talked to the garage earlier. It's not just a faulty starter motor. There's all kinds of problems under that hood. They say I should trade the car in.'

'Can we afford to do that, Frank?'

'Looks like we might have to. I must have a reliable car.'

'Yes, of course.'

His tone brightened. 'How are the boys?'

'Full of beans. Charging around the garden.'

'That sounds like them.'

'Mike is pleased with himself because Miss Jaglan pinned up one of his drawings on the wall of his classroom.'

'Not that one of me, I hope!' said Frank in alarm. 'You know, the one that made me look like Spock out of *Star Trek*.'

They shared a laugh and talked for a little longer about their sons. Then Frank told her that he had to get back to his work.

'How will you get back?' she asked.

'I'll take the train.'

'The early one?'

'No, I have a few things to do here. I'll probably get the 6:25.'

'Shall I meet you at the station?'

'No thanks. I'll grab a taxi.'

'Hurry home.'

'Yeah.'

'I love you,' she whispered.

'I love you, too,' he replied with routine affection.

Ann put the receiver down and went back to her chores. Frank looked up at the clock on the wall and saw that it was five o'clock. He reached for some paperwork and got stuck into it. His interest soon waned. He made another effort but he was somehow unable to concentrate. He kept seeing the auburn hair in front of him and hearing Ed Lasky's voice buzzing in his ear.

'So what are you going to do about it?'

Frank put his papers aside and buzzed the intercom. As he was gathering up his things, Leona came into the office. She was wearing the perfume he had given her for Christmas.

'Yes, Mr Raftis?'

'I'm leaving. What have we got?'

'Herring-Landau.'

'I'll call them tomorrow.'

'Harry Stingler, Victor Rawlins and your wife.'

'I just talked to her. The rest can wait.'

'But . . .'

'I've got to run.'

And he was gone. Leona raised her eyebrows in surprise. It was most unlike her boss to behave like that. Was anything wrong?

Frank made it to Grand Central Station by half-past five and waited in the queue at the information desk. Eventually, his turn came. He had deduced that she must live further along the line than Dobbs Ferry and his guess was an accurate one.

'What time is the next train to Ardsley?'

'Five forty-seven. Gate 24.'

'And after that?'

'Six-oh-three, six twenty-five . . .'

'And after that?'

'How many trains you catching, mister?' wondered the clerk.

'Please. It's important. Give me two more.'

'Six forty-seven, seven-oh-three. That good enough for you?'

'Thanks . . .'

69

He sprinted through the crowd to Gate 24.

The main concourse was a turmoil of bodies as thousands of commuters streamed towards their respective trains, showing far more urgency to leave Manhattan than they did to come into it. Frank lurked near the relevant gate and tried to make himself as inconspicuous as possible. At the same time, he scrutinized every face that went past him in the hope that hers might be among them. But he watched in vain. Whatever train she was catching, it was certainly not the first one.

He relaxed for a few minutes and talked to himself.

'Hi, how are you . . . Well, hi . . . Well, hello again. What a surprise. No, I was just . . . Listen, I was wondering if . . .'

He suddenly felt ridiculous and cut short his rehearsal. What, after all, was he doing there? Waiting for someone who would probably not come and who might not care to speak to him anyway. The odds against his meeting her were huge. She might have taken an earlier train or be travelling home by car. It was even possible that she was staying the night in Manhattan.

What *was* he doing there? Frank could not find a satisfactory answer. Nor could he tear himself away, however. When the passengers surged through the gate towards the next train, he was on duty once more to check them all out. No luck. No auburn hair. No hope.

'Listen, I didn't get your name this morning . . . My name is Frank Raftis . . . Do you . . .?'

It sounded better. He went through it a dozen times.

Passengers thrust past him in droves yet again and he went through the same vigil. Nothing. She was obviously not going to come. He glanced up at the clock and was startled to realize that he had been on duty at the gate for over three-quarters of an hour. The train he had himself planned to catch was now rapidly filling up. To wait any longer would be to risk missing it completely.

Frank gave up. He went quickly through the gate and down on to the platform, scolding himself for his stupidity in believing that she would turn up, realizing how absurd he must have looked skulking there and searching anxiously among the faces. As he got into the train and walked down the car, he felt foolish, disappointed and very selfconscious. He was glad to drop into a seat and hide behind his newspaper. It was then that he experienced another sensation. Pain. Wounded pride. Damaged self-esteem.

It was almost as if he had been jilted.

Molly Gilmore, meanwhile, was breaking into a trot across the main concourse. The clock told her that she had two minutes before the train departed and she feared that she would not get to it in time. She charged through the gate, went down to the platform and lengthened her stride. Seconds after she climbed aboard, the train was in motion. She leaned against the door for a few moments to recover her breath and then went into the first car. All the seats were taken. Molly went through into the next car and that, too, was full. But she did not leave immediately.

She had seen him and something tingled inside her.

He was reading his newspaper just a few seats away from her and she could not take her eyes off him. The conductor walked down the aisle towards her.

'There are more seats forward, Ma'am.'

'Oh. Thanks. Yes.'

She went on through into the next car, wondering if she should have spoken to Frank, wishing that he had at least looked up to see her. Now it was too late. They were on the same train but they might as well be miles apart. She plonked herself down on a seat and blamed herself for missing the chance to make contact with him again.

Without knowing it, however, she had made contact. Frank had recognized her voice when she spoke to the conductor and had glanced up in time to see her going out. His immediate impulse was to follow her and he turned to the man sitting outside him.

'Excuse me.'

'Sure . . .'

The man stood up to let Frank past and the latter stepped out into the aisle. Doubts now began to assail him. What right did he have to go after her and what would he say when he got there? In any case, how could they possibly have a private conversation on a crowded train? He swung back to the man.

'Excuse me. Sorry . . . I . . . sorry.'

'Make up your mind, will you?'

Frank resumed his seat as the man stood up to let him through. The train roared on through the evening until it came to its first stop. Now behind his paper again, Frank mused on the irony of the situation. He had waited almost an hour for her and she did not show up, yet now she was in the next car and he was afraid to go to her. It was ludicrous. He turned to the window and looked out at the gathering sunset. The train continued to race.

'Dobbs Ferry! Next stop – Dobbs Ferry!'

The conductor's voice stirred him into action. He folded his newspaper, gathered up his things, apologized again to his neighbour, went out into the aisle and moved along the car. It was all over. What was probably his only chance of another meeting with her had been squandered. Frank sighed and shuffled out through the door.

Molly Gilmore was right in front of him. She was standing beside an open window between the cars and gazing out. Cool air was rushing in. She was framed by a small rectangle of sunset.

'You can have my seat,' he offered.

She turned to face him. They both smiled involuntarily.

'Oh. No. Hi. No, that's alright. I'm . . . I'm fine.'

'Oh. I saw you.'

'Yes. I just wanted some air.'

'You're sure?'

'Yes.'

'If you change your mind . . .'

'It's O.K. I have a seat in the other car.'

'Oh.'

'Yes.'

'I see.'

'Thanks, anyway.'

There was an embarrassed pause. Frank ran through all the lines he had rehearsed and rejected them without even trying them. His legs told him to move away but his hand suddenly thrust itself out towards her.

'Frank Raftis.'

She shook his hand. 'Hello again.'

'Yeah.'

His legs were getting restless again. Time to go.

'Margaret,' she blurted out. 'Margaret Gilmore.'

'Margaret, eh?'

'Well, Molly.'

'Do you work in the city?'

'No, I'm married.' She had not meant it to sound so defensive.

'Oh.'

'I mean, no, I don't work. I mean, I do work but I'm not working right now. That's about it, I guess.'

'Oh.'

'Do you?' she asked, nervously.

'What? Work?'

'In the city.'

'Oh. Yes.'

'My father is ill. I've been coming in a lot. To see him.'

73

'I'm sorry.'

'Every day, in fact. To the hospital.'

'It's serious, then?'

She nodded away. 'Far more serious than he'll ever admit. My father is one of those people who never accept that there can be anything wrong with them. You know? Also, he has this thing about doctors so he's giving them a pretty bad time up at that hospital. The world's worst patient. I bet they'll be glad to see the back of him. He can be so difficult.' Molly stopped herself. Why was she gabbling like this? Why not tell him what she really wanted to say? 'I thought about you today,' she admitted.

Frank was delighted. 'You did?'

'Yes. I mean, seeing you again. I mean, well, you know, seeing you again after so many months.'

'Yeah. Funny.'

'Yes.'

There was another pause as they studied each other's faces more closely. Frank loved the curve of her cheek.

'I'm married, too,' he confessed.

'Well, lots of people are.'

'Yeah, I guess so.'

They exchanged another smile and felt more relaxed.

'Is your wife the gardener?'

'What? Oh, the book.'

'Gardening For All Seasons . . .'

'Yes. She . . . uh, yes. Sort of.'

'I see.'

'And your husband? Is he the . . .?'

'Well, he's interested in sailing, yes. The idea of it, that is. Never seems to have any time to do it, I'm afraid, but . . . yes, the book was for him.'

Frank was gazing steadily at her, quite unaware of the fact that the train was slowing as it came into Dobbs Ferry Station. Molly glanced over her shoulder.

'You're going to miss your stop,' she warned.

'Yeah. Listen. Are you, do you, will you be coming in tomorrow?'

'No.'

'Oh.'

'No,' she repeated, softly.

'Yeah.' He gestured awkwardly. 'I'm not . . . This is not . . . I'm not trying to . . .'

'No. I know.'

'I thought we could . . . maybe we could ride together.'

'Oh.'

'OK. Well . . . I'm sorry. I didn't mean . . .'

The conductor walked past them calling loudly.

'Dobbs Ferry. Station stop is Dobbs Ferry. Please exit forward.'

Frank had to go. 'Well . . .'

'Nine fifteen,' she heard herself saying.

'What?'

'I usually catch the nine fifteen.'

His smile returned. 'OK. Great. Yeah. OK.'

'OK.' she agreed.

And he rushed off towards the exit.

Molly remained at the window long enough to see him step out on to the platform and wave back to her, then she went into the tiny bathroom between the cars. She was so dizzy and out of breath that she had to sit down on the toilet seat. She ran cold water into the basin and splashed it over her face and neck.

She had arranged to meet him. It was a form of assignation. Molly was at once shocked at her boldness and pleased with her instinct. But the pressure of conflicting emotions was too much for her and she felt as if she was on the point of retching.

The train picked up speed and left Dobbs Ferry behind.

Frank Raftis climbed into the car beside his wife.

75

'You didn't have to pick me up.'

'Hi, Dad!'

'Have a good day, Dad!'

'Hi, Mike . . . Hi, Joe,' he called to the boys on the back seat. 'No problem for me to take a cab, Ann.'

'I don't mind,' she said, driving away. 'The garage called. Your car is ready. We can pick it up on the way.'

'Leave it,' he decided. 'I'll get it at the weekend.'

'Why?'

'It's too much trouble. I'm going to take the train in for a while.'

Ann shrugged. 'OK.'

Frank turned round and began to chat to his sons.

Molly Gilmore lay curled up on the sofa with a book in her lap. It had been open at the same page for over ten minutes and she was not even pretending to look at it. Her mind was still on the train.

Brian came out of the kitchen and walked up behind her. When he kissed her on the top of the head, she jumped in surprise and all but threw the book on the floor.

'Take it easy,' he cautioned.

'Oh. Sorry.'

'Where were you?'

'Nowhere.'

'Miles away.'

'Tired,' she explained.

'You can sleep in tomorrow. Catch up.'

'No. I'm going into the city.'

'I thought you were staying home for once.'

'Yeah. But I think I'd better. He didn't look so good today, Brian. I want to go back.'

'You're too kind,' he observed.

'No, I'm not.'

He kissed her again. 'I'm turning in.'

'I'll be right there . . .'

'Say, what did you do in Manhattan all day?' he asked, pausing in the doorway. 'You weren't at the hospital all the time, were you?'

'No. I had lunch with Isabelle.'

'Oh.'

'She thinks I should go back to work.'

'What's the point, Molly?'

'I'm only telling you what she thinks.'

'Do you *want* to go back?'

'I don't know, Brian.'

'That means no, then,' he said, firmly. 'See you upstairs . . .'

He went out and Molly glanced down at the book.

'Don't be long!' he called from the landing.

His wife did not even hear him. She was too busy thinking about the colourful pullover she had bought for Christmas and which she had been forced to exchange for a dull, uneventful cardigan. The pullover had not suited Brian at all but on Frank Raftis it would look good. It had been the right garment. For the wrong man.

She was still thinking about Frank as she fell asleep.

They dropped the children off at school and then swung back to pick up the main road again. Ann was conscious of her passenger's suppressed irritation and she could not understand it.

'Do you want me to drive?' asked Frank.

'No.'

'I'd go much faster,' he badgered.

'What *is* the matter with you?'

'I'm late.'

'Then why didn't you take an earlier train?' she countered. 'You were up. Ready. You've been up since the crack of dawn.'

'I couldn't sleep.'

'Why not?'

'Who knows?'

'Frank, is everything alright?'

'Of course, it is. What a stupid question!' He saw that he had hurt her feelings and took a deep breath. 'Look, I'm sorry, Ann. I feel a bit tense, that's all.'

'You'll catch your train,' she said, coldly.

'I don't want an argument.'

'Who's arguing?'

'I'm in a hurry. That's what's wrong with me.'

'Is that why you were so angry with Mike and Joe?'

'Ann . . .'

'Well, is it? Is it?'

'They were holding us up.'

'Frank, they have to go to school!'

'I knew I should have taken a cab,' he muttered, ruefully.

'And what's so special about this train? Why are you in such a panic to catch it?' She stole a look at him. 'Answer me!'

'Do you want me to drive or not?'

By way of a reply, she pressed her foot down hard on the accelerator. Frank glared through the windscreen and brooded.

Molly Gilmore put her handbag on the seat next to her in order to reserve it. She had bought a newspaper at the station but found that her hands were trembling when she tried to read it. The train seemed to take an age to reach Dobbs Ferry. Her head craned at the window as they drew up alongside the platform and then her stomach turned.

He was not there. She had so confidently assumed that he would be waiting that she was now completely taken aback. Frank had changed his mind. He did not want to see her again, after all. Molly settled back in her seat and folded her hands in her lap. The train was soon in motion again. Her hopes withered.

'Is this seat taken?' asked a man's voice.

'Yes!' she replied, firmly.

'Oh.'

She looked up and saw bewilderment on Frank's face. He was standing in the aisle beside her. Molly laughed with relief and moved her handbag from the adjoining seat.

'I mean . . . yes. Yes, it *is* taken. Now.' He sat down gratefully. 'I didn't see you on the platform.'

'Almost missed it.'

'I'm glad you didn't.'

'Me, too.'

'Well . . .' That warm feeling had come back to her now.

'OK.?' he asked.

'OK.'

They smiled in unison. The journey was far too short for all that they wanted to pack into it. Each had stored up dozens of questions to ask the other and the words came tumbling out.

'You said that you worked, Molly.'

'I used to.'

'What as?'

'Graphic designer.'

He was impressed. 'Hey's that's good!'

'Advertising.'

'Madison Avenue?'

'Citicorp, actually. My last job. You?'

'Architectural engineer.'

'Wow!'

'It's not as important as it sounds.'

'Oh, come on! Do you like it?'

'Love it.'

'I'm sure . . .'

The train was already emerging from the tunnel into Grand Central Station. They could not believe they had arrived in Manhattan and felt cheated. On the walk along the platform, the questions continued to flow unabated.

'. . . which hospital is your father in?'

'. . . what project are you on at the moment?'

'. . . long have you lived in Ardsley?'

'. . . Dobbs Ferry nice?'

'. . . who's Isabelle?'

'. . . Ed?'

They had reached the main concourse before she got around to his children. He told her that he had two sons.

'How old?'

'Mike is six and Joe is four . . . no, five. Had a birthday only last month.'

'Really?'

'We took him to the circus.'

'I bet he loved that!'

'Yeah. Only trouble is, we've got to take Mike to a circus on *his* birthday now. What about you, Molly?'

'Always liked the circus.'

'I meant kids. Do you have any?'

'No.'

'Oh.'

'We decided against it . . .' They were out in the street now and she was looking around. 'I need a cab.'

'I'll get it.'

Frank ran into the road and waved a taxi down. He opened the door for Molly to get in. She was still asking questions to the last. Neither of them could stop laughing.

After a while, the driver's patience showed signs of wear and tear.

'You want to go somewhere or don't you?'

'Oh sure,' said Molly.

Frank leaned in. 'Six twenty-five?'

'Six twenty-five,' she confirmed.

'Have a nice day.'

'And you.'

'Bye.'

'Bye . . .'

Molly waved as Frank went back to the sidewalk. He started to walk, then trot, then almost bound along with sheer high spirits. The cab driver got a glimpse of him in his wing mirror.

'That your husband?'

'No.'

'Thought not.'

His grin was cynical. He had seen it all before.

'Where to, lady?'

Chapter 6

The construction site was one vast cauldron of noise and activity. Cranes swung, concrete slurped, hammers banged, engines chugged, voices yelled and riveters pecked away monotonously at steel. A ship's siren added to the cacophony as the vessel glided past on the East River. Heavy lorries arrived with fresh supplies. The elevator clanged up and down the side of the building. Somewhere a pneumatic drill was testing its lungs.

It was a normal day on site. Frank Raftis and Vic Rawlins strolled towards one of the trailers as if the barrage of noise did not exist. Vic was doing most of the talking.

'I can up the fee and they're willing to throw in a house. Do you hear that, Frank? A nice big house for the wife and kids. All ready and waiting.'

'It will have to wait.'

'I can't believe this is you talking.'

'Vic, I got things to keep me here.'

'What things?'

'Work.'

'*This* is work. Highly-paid work.'

'Yeah. In Houston.'

'What the hell have you got against Houston all of a sudden? I bet you've never even been near the place?'

'You're right. I haven't. And I won't.'

'Six months ago, you'd have jumped at this opportunity.'

'Things change.'

'Not that much. Something's happened to you, Frank.'

'Yeah. I started to enjoy living in Dobbs Ferry.'

'Nobody's trying to take your house *off* you. It'll be there when you come back.'

'But I'm not going anywhere.'

Vic put a hand on his shoulder to stop him then grimaced as another vessel blew its siren out in the river. He stepped closer to Frank and gave him a shrewd stare.

'Have you discussed this with Ann?' he asked.

'No point.'

'Unilateral rejection, eh?'

'She doesn't want to move any more than I do.'

'She's moved before and so have you. It goes with the territory. You can't expect the big chances to pop up right on your doorstep.'

'I know that.'

'You telling me you're only interested in working here?'

'No, Vic. It's not that . . .'

'Then what is it, for Christ's sake.' He took him by the shoulders. 'What are you holding out for?'

'Nothing.'

'More dough? A car? A bigger slice of the action?'

Frank sighed and shook his head. 'Look, I appreciate what you're trying to do for me. It's a great opportunity, I can see that. But it just doesn't have my name on it. Simple as that.'

'*Put* your name on it, Frank.'

'Sorry.'

'Okay. I will. In pencil.'

'You'll need to rub it out.'

'We'll see,' returned the other, confidently. 'You've never turned me down yet, Frank, and you're not going to start now. I'll keep the job on ice for a while. You'll come round.'

'Don't put money on that, Vic.'

'Of course, the other thing about Houston . . .'

'Another time, Vic. I have to make a call. OK?'

He turned on his heel and continued on towards the trailer. The architect watched for a moment then yelled after him.

'I won't give up on you, Frank!'

'Thanks,' came the reply.

'Sonofabitch,' muttered Vic to himself.

Frank went into the trailer and crossed to the telephone. He took off his hard hat, fished out a piece of paper from his shirt pocket, and began to dial the number written on it. He suddenly stopped and put the receiver down again. Pacing to and fro in the small office, he checked his watch and pondered. He soon decided.

This time he almost jumped to the telephone.

John Trainer sat in his bed at Lenox Hill Hospital and laughed for the first time in months. Molly was telling him a joke and she was thrilled to hear his rich chuckle once again.

'Wait a minute,' she said, 'you haven't heard the punchline yet. This'll really kill you!'

'Go on, then.'

'. . . and the little girl says "Do you want to kiss it?" And the little boy says "Well, I'm not *really* a racer."'

It was not the best or the subtlest joke that he had ever heard but it made him laugh out loud. He was still shaking with mirth when the telephone rang. Molly crossed to it.

'Hello?'

'Molly?' It was him.

'Oh. Hi.'

'Hope you don't mind me calling you there?'

'If it's for me,' said her father, 'tell them I'm not here.'

'Molly?' Frank's voice sounded very distant.

'No, no, it's alright,' she assured him.

'Hey, listen. I'm going to be near the hospital in about half an hour. Any chance of seeing you?'

'Well . . .'

'Who is it?' asked her father.

'Say, around twelve-thirty?'

'Molly, who *is* it?'

'Yes,' she agreed. 'Yes . . . yes.'

'See you outside the main entrance.'

'OK.'

Frank rang off and she put down the receiver, wondering if she had done the right thing. Her father was beckoning her over. She went back to the bed and sat down again.

'For you?' he asked. She nodded. 'Not him?'

'Him?'

'Your husband. Burt.'

'*Brian*. And no, it wasn't him.'

'Then who?'

'Nobody you know.'

'Hey, this is my room. My telephone. I don't want complete strangers ringing up. Why did you give out the number?'

'I didn't . . . Now, relax. What was I saying?'

'The joke . . . little boy, little girl . . .'

'Oh yes. I know another one like that. Even better . . .'

Molly kept up the jokes and bright talk until her father began to doze off again. His jaw sagged when he slept and his whole body seemed to collapse inwards. His skin had become sallow. She gazed fondly at him and wondered how much weight he had lost since he came into hospital. Asleep, off guard, in the harsh light, he looked dreadful.

She was glad when it was time to leave.

Frank was waiting for her outside. When he saw her

coming, he took his hands out of his pockets and strode over to her.

'Hi. Sorry.'

'What?'

'Nothing. Uh. Do you . . . Do you want to have lunch?'

She was flustered. 'Oh I don't know . . . I mean . . .'

'You're very beautiful.'

'No. No, I'm not,' she denied. 'I'm very married.'

'Yeah. Me, too. But even married people have to eat.'

Molly hesitated. It seemed like too big a commitment too soon. But she *was* hungry. And the sun was very warm. And Frank was so boyishly eager that she did not have the heart to disappoint him.

She flashed him her best smile.

They had lunch at an outdoor cafe and picked up where they had left off, firing questions at each other as fast as they could. He was fascinated by her work as a graphic artist and asked if he could see examples of what she had done. Molly, in turn, was intrigued by the whole world of construction as explained by him and could have listened all afternoon.

When the meal was over, they strolled along Park Avenue with an ice cream cone apiece. Frank pointed ahead.

'This avenue was a solid granite ridge. All the way down. Nobody could live here. Then the railroad blasted a deep cut right down the middle. Ran the trains through it. But still nobody lived here, because of the smoke and dirt. Just some people in shacks. It wasn't until the turn of the century, the trains were electrified and the street was covered over . . .' He stopped and turned to her. 'You're letting me talk like this because you don't want to talk about yourself.'

'That's not true.'

'Prove it,' he challenged.

'OK. What do you want to know?'

'Everything.'

Brian Gilmore drove down a leafy suburban road and turned into the drive of an imposing house. No sooner had he stopped then the front door of the house opened and a distraught woman in her thirties came rushing out to meet him.

'Oh, I'm so glad you're here at last, Doctor Gilmore!'

'How is she, Mrs Shaffer?'

'Weaker than ever.'

'Is she eating anything?'

'Not really.'

'And those tablets I prescribed?'

'Yes, yes. She's been taking those.'

Brian was ushered into the hall and up the stairs to the child's room. It was done out in yellow and white wallpaper that was patterned with characters from nursery rhymes. Baby toys were everywhere. The child was lying in its cot. Brian put down his bag then lowered the side of the cot to get at the patient.

The anxious father had now joined his wife and both parents watched as Brian went through a routine sequence of tests. The child submitted to being handled and seemed to have no strength to protest. Brian's eyes darkened with professional concern.

'Well, doctor?' asked the mother.

'Is she going to be alright? pressed her husband.

'You were right to call me,' Brian told them.

'It's her breathing,' said Mrs Shaffer. 'It sounded . . . well, not right somehow. Is she . . . is she . . .?'

'I want Ruth to go into hospital for a few days.'

'Hospital!' She quailed and her husband put a steadying arm around her shoulders. 'Is it *that* serious.'

'Only for observation,' Brian assured her. 'They have all the equipment there. Ruth will be in the best possible place.'

'We'll be guided by you, doctor,' said Mr Shaffer.

'When will she have to go?' asked his wife.

'As soon as possible. If I could have the use of a 'phone . . .'

'This way, doctor,' invited Mr Shaffer.

Brian was led into the master bedroom and left alone to make his call. When he had contacted the hospital and made the necessary arrangements, he glanced round to make sure that he was not overheard. Then he dialled his home number and told Molly that he would be back a little later than expected that evening.

Frank Raftis poured over some plans spread out on his drawing board and made a few pencilled notes on a pad. There was a knock on the door and Leona entered with a mug of coffee for him. He glanced at his watch, saw the time and abandoned his work.

'Thanks for the coffee, Leona, but I'll have to leave it.'

'Why, Mr Raftis?'

'An appointment. I'm going out.'

'Now?' She could remember nothing in his diary.

'You have the coffee for me.'

'But what time will you be back?'

'Search me . . .'

He went out through the door and left her justifiably piqued. It was not the first time in the past two weeks that he had suddenly dropped everything and charged out of the office. Leona looked at the coffee in annoyance then began to sip it disconsolately.

Frank, meanwhile, stepped into the street to find that it

was pouring with rain. Molly was waiting for him in the doorway, huddled under a newspaper that was already soaking wet.

'Hope you didn't mind me ringing you, Frank.'

'Of course not. Had a free hour to kill.'

'Then let's kill it!'

Sheltering together under the newspaper, they went out into the road to try to hail a taxi but all they got for their pains was a further splashing of water from the hissing tyres of passing vehicles. They decided to go for a bus and rushed around the corner to Madison Avenue. A bus was pulling away from the stop and, though Frank banged manfully on the doors, they would not open.

'We must get out of this rain,' he said.

'Do you know the Frick Collection?'

'The what?'

'Good. Follow me.'

The place was a revelation to Frank. He had been past it countless times and admired its elegance but he had never realized the range and quality of the art treasures that it contained. Molly was in her element, guiding him around, identifying the paintings at a glance and telling him all the anecdotes associated with them. They began in the Boucher Room and worked their way steadily around the whole house. By the time they reached the West Gallery, they had dried off completely.

The room was decorated with sixteenth century Italian furniture and exquisite Persian carpets. Portraits and landscapes of the Dutch, French, Spanish and British schools were hung with taste and reverence. Molly stood beside one of the three Rembrandt paintings on display.

'This is a self-portrait,' she announced.

'What were you saying back there about the eyes?' he asked.

'Oh that. The idea is that one eye projects and the other

eye receives. Try it. Cover your right eye and look at the painting.'

Molly demonstrated, putting a hand over her right eye. Frank followed suit but kept his left eye firmly on her. She laughed.

'No. Look at the *painting*.'

'Am I projecting or receiving?'

The Frick Collection was fun. When they came out again, the rain had stopped and the sun had come out. They walked until they found somewhere to have a cup of coffee. Molly had started to tell him about her parents.

'They made a lot of noise. No matter what they were doing. Fighting, having a good time, making love. Lots of noise. It was terrifying. I never understood it. I was always afraid they were going to get a divorce and go away. So I got quieter. That's how I grew up. Quiet. Inoffensive. Shy.' She stirred her coffee. 'Now I admire them. For *feeling* that much. For letting it all out. I can't do that, Frank.'

'Why not? What are you afraid of?'

'I don't know. I suppose I'm afraid everybody will go away if I make too much noise.' She looked at him. 'If I *feel* too much.'

'*I* won't go away,' he promised.

That evening they shared a train ride home once more.

Ann Raftis sat in her kitchen and went through her list of jobs for the day. There was a lot to be fitted in before she picked up the children from school. One of her calls was to the dry cleaner's and she was astonished to see how many items her husband had left to be taken along. Among them was a pair of grey trousers that he had only worn once or twice since their last visit to the cleaner's. It was all completely out of character for him. Frank usually had to be bullied into letting his clothes be dry cleaned.

Ann was baffled by this change in her husband, as she was by a few other changes. Why, for instance, had he stopped driving into the city? In the past, he had always complained that the train was too crowded and inconvenient for him yet now he took it every day.

As Ann worked her way down her list, there was more than one thing that required a few words with Frank. She stockpiled her queries and then rang him at the office.

Leona's voice answered with easy politeness.

'Can I speak to my husband, please, Leona?' asked Ann.

'I'm afraid not, Mrs Raftis. He's not in the office.'

'Could I get him on site?'

'He isn't there either.'

'A business appointment?'

'You might call it that. Mr Raftis is at the gymnasium.'

'The gym? But it's only mid-morning.'

'That's where he is . . .'

Ann thanked her and rang off. She now had more cause for concern.

Ed Lasky punished himself with the heavy weights. Lying on his back, he forced the bar up until his arms straightened, then controlled the downward movement. There was no respite. His arms were on fire and his shoulders aching painfully but he forced himself to carry on. Sweat ran down his face like a small waterfall. His stomach churned.

'Masochist!'

'Hi, Frank.'

'How much longer you going to keep that up?'

'I'm not a quitter like you.'

'What do you mean?' argued Frank. 'I've just had a terrific workout. I feel great.'

Ed managed a few more lifts then dropped the weights

91

back into position with a resounding clang. He was panting badly and needed a few seconds before he could speak.

'Who's idea was it to come here, anyway?' he complained.

'Mine,' accepted Frank.

'And why?'

'I just felt like some exercise, that's all.'

'That's all, he says! I wasn't born yesterday, Frank.' He slid forwards under the bar then sat up to face his friend. 'Come on. What's her name?'

'Whose name?'

'I been playing these games a lot longer than you, remember. I can spot the signs. So tell me – who is she?'

'You got it all wrong, Ed.'

'Who *is* she!'

There was a pause. 'Nobody you know . . . and before you say anything, it's not like that . . . Why are you grinning?'

'Because I remembered. It's her, isn't it?'

'Who?'

'On the train.'

'Ed . . .'

'Christmas Eve in Rizzoli's!'

'Now, listen . . .'

'So you finally got up enough guts to do something about it! That's the best news I've had all day. Well done, Frank.' He rolled his eyes. 'What's she like in the sack?'

'Knock it off, will you!' said Frank, angrily.

'Hey, hey there. Now cool it, man,' advised his friend. 'No need to be so uptight about it. I'm sorry. OK? I'm sorry. Had no idea it was as serious as that.'

'As what?'

'You're in real deep, aren't you?'

'I got to go back to the office . . .'

Ed held his arm. 'Pull yourself together, Frank. So it's special for you. Good. It was like that for me and Carol at first.'

Frank resented the comparison but he reined in his temper. In his own peculiar way, Ed Lasky was trying to help him even though Ed was ignorant of the situation. Frank tried to keep calm.

'Nothing's happened so far, has it?' probed Ed.

'Well . . .'

'I thought not. You or her?'

'Look . . .'

'Know what you should do? Take her to a hotel.'

'I told you. It's not like that!'

'Okay, an apartment, then. Borrow mine, if you like. But for God's sakes, take her somewhere soon, Frank, or you're going to explode. I mean – hell! – what are you saving it for?'

It was pointless to try to explain to him. Frank went off to the showers and let the cold water play on him for a long time.

Molly Gilmore had never let herself be pampered quite so much before. She had a facial, a manicure, a pedicure and a new hairstyle. On Isabelle's recommendation ('It's so damn sexy, honey') she even tried aromatherapy, a form of deep massage using essential oils. She came out of it all looking good and feeling on top of the world. The transformation delighted Frank but it did not meet with universal approval.

'What have you done to yourself?'

'I had my hair done, Brian. That's all.'

'Why?'

'I was ready for a change.'

'Oh.'

'Don't you like it?'

'I liked it the way it was before.'

'You'll get used to it.'

They were dining at home one evening. Brian had drunk slightly too much wine and it made him unpredictable. Molly was not sure what he was going to say or do next. They ate in silence until he had cleared his plate. He jerked his head up as if she had spoken.

'Hm?'

'Nothing . . .'

'I thought . . .'

An even longer silence followed. Molly was about to clear the things away when Brian sighed. He stared into space.

'The Shaffer baby died today.'

'Oh no.'

'Yes.'

'I'm sorry.'

'Well,' said Brian with casual indifference. 'Life and death. Seems to be a lot of that going around these days. Not that it matters. Not that it makes a hell of a lot of difference. We're used to it. Roll 'em in. Roll 'em out. Do what you can. Say something nice to the parents – "Terrible loss. Terrible". Don't feel responsible. Don't feel guilty. Don't feel *anything*!'

'Brian . . .'

'Well, the truth is, I don't. I don't, Molly. I don't feel a thing.' He stared across at her. 'Do you want to go to a movie?'

Molly shook her head. He got up and went out. She sat there quietly appalled at what he had said. He had gone into the medical profession with such high ideals and with such compassion. She had been attracted by his sense of commitment, by his zeal for medicine as a way to serve the community. Yet now he was talking like this. What had happened to him? What had happened to her?

She heard him padding around in the other room and had a strong feeling that she wanted to keep out of his way. Dinner with her husband was no longer the pleasant ritual it had always been.

What was happening to *them*?

The train on the Metro North Commuter Railroad was a silver and blue flash as it streaked south through Westchester County. Riding between the cars, a man and a woman were able to enjoy sufficient privacy to talk about an intensely personal matter.

'So you did have a child?' said Frank.

'Yes. Just the one. A boy.' Molly's voice was toneless. 'He was only a few weeks old. Nobody's fault. Except Brian thought . . . felt it was his fault. I mean, he's a doctor.'

'Sure . . .'

'I thought, well, we *should* have.'

'But you didn't.'

'No.'

'Children.'

'Yes.'

A passenger came out to use the bathroom and they fell silent immediately. Frank looked down into her troubled face.

'Why haven't you told me this before?' he asked.

'I didn't know you properly.'

'Or trust me.'

'That, too.'

'But you trust me now?'

She nodded. 'Also . . .'

'Go on.'

'Well, it's something I try to forget. Push out of my mind. I pretend that it never happened.' She heaved a

95

sigh. 'But it *did* happen, of course. And it's always there between us somehow. Between Brian and me.'

'You might still have children,' he said.

'I doubt it.'

'You can't live without hope, Molly. Nobody can live without some kind of hope.'

'I don't know. Sometimes . . . I don't know.'

'No,' he emphasized. 'You can't live without hope.'

When they reached their destination, they followed their now established pattern of walking through the concourse together and out into the street where Frank hailed a taxi for her. Molly felt protected when she was with him. Cared for and looked after. As the taxi carried her away, she was glad that she had told him about her baby. It was something she could no longer even discuss with Brian.

Her first call was at Isabelle's office.

'I don't know what you've been up to but you look terrific!' said her friend, approvingly. 'Like a million dollars!'

'I do? Well, I feel good. I've been going to the gym.'

'The gym?'

'You know, workouts. Aerobics.'

'That's not what I'd call it, Molly!'

'What . . .?'

'I think it goes by the name of good, old-fashioned sex.'

'Isabelle!'

'You can't fool me, honey. I knew something was up when you asked me about aromatherapy at that Beauty Clinic. Now come on. Own up. Who is it?'

'Who is what?'

'You're seeing somebody, aren't you?'

Molly panicked. 'Sorry. I have to go.'

'But you've only just got here.'

'The hospital. I have to visit my father.'

'We haven't looked at your drawings yet,' argued Isabelle, indicating the folder that Molly had brought with her. 'You can't dash off until I've seen these.'

'Well, alright . . .'

Molly undid the fastening on the folder and opened it. Inside were half a dozen design ideas for advertisements. Isabelle took them out and cast a professional eye over them.

'When did you do these?' she wondered.

'In my spare time.'

'Always beats me. How can you be so timid in real life and yet so aggressive when you pick up a brush? These are good. Very good. Tough, ballsy, bags of colour.' She held one up to examine it more closely. 'I could just see this on a hoarding somewhere. You still got that flair, Molly.'

'Thanks.'

'So when are you coming back to work?'

'I'm not.'

'You're going to let all this talent go to waste?'

'I'm not ready to come back yet.'

'Why not?'

Molly put the drawings back in the folder. 'I'm too busy.'

'Too busy doing *what*?' asked Isabelle, meaningfully.

'I really must run . . .'

'At least tell me his name.'

'I can't. Sorry.'

'Molly, what *is* going on!'

'He's a friend, that's all,' said Molly, almost gabbling. 'We have lunch sometimes. I like him. He makes me feel good. I like seeing him. I like thinking about him. We do things. We laugh. That's all. I don't even know him really. I just like being with him. I like to . . . I like . . . Oh, god!'

The rush of thoughts was too powerful for her and tears welled up in her eyes. Isabelle at once tried to put her arms around her friend but Molly backed away.

'I must go.'

'You listen to me . . .'

Molly suddenly hugged her very tightly.

'No. No, Isabelle. Please. I don't want to listen. I'll call you tomorrow. Please. OK?'

Before Isabelle could reply, Molly had gone.

Chapter 7

The yellow cab drew up outside the main entrance to the hospital. Molly Gilmore got out with a smile on her face, paid the driver and tipped him handsomely. She was in good spirits and her face was quite radiant. When she had first started to visit the hospital on a regular basis, she had found it rather grim and depressing but familiarity had given it an altogether warmer and more welcoming aspect. The building had a reassuring solidity about it. In the hands of the medical staff, she somehow felt, her father was very safe.

She took the elevator to the third floor and walked along the spotlessly clean corridor, her heels clacking on the shining surface. The problem of cheering her father up no longer seemed an onerous chore. Molly was in a mood to tell him jokes and funny stories for hours on end. She turned a corner and positively skipped towards his room.

'Mrs Gilmore?'

'Yes?'

'I wonder if I might have a word?'

The doctor intercepted her before she reached the door. He had the calm, neutral expression of someone who is about to impart bad news. Molly knew that expression well. Brian wore it every day. She asked herself if it was something doctors were taught at medical school.

'How is he, doctor?'

'Rather poorly.'

'Since when?'

'Last night. His condition worsened.'

'Oh.' Her spirits had now dropped completely.

'It's still not critical yet but . . .'

'You want to operate,' she guessed.

'Yes.'

'Is it really necessary?'

'I'm afraid so. A by-pass operation.'

'He won't like that one bit!' she warned.

'He doesn't have much choice.'

She nodded. 'Have you told him yet?'

'No, not yet.'

'He so hates the idea of having surgery.'

'We all do, Mrs Gilmore.'

'What? Oh yes . . .'

The doctor almost smiled. 'Your father has been very good to this hospital. Very generous. In view of that, it's surprising that he's been such a difficult patient.'

'It was protection money.'

'I beg your pardon?'

'My father's donations. Protection money. He was paying it to you so that you'd never come and get him. But you did.'

The doctor looked at her shrewdly and Molly wished that she had not made the quip. Then she realized that it had not been her talking but her father. She had answered for *him*. It said something for the bond between them.

'Anything we can do . . .' began the doctor.

'Yes, thanks . . . thanks . . . I'd better . . .'

'He's heavily sedated.'

'I must see him, doctor.'

'There's not really much point if he's . . .'

'I just want to see him,' she insisted.

The man nodded and stepped out of her way.

Molly let herself into the room and went slowly across to the bed. Her father had drifted off into a deep sleep. His body was totally limp and his mouth was agape.

Against the starched whiteness of the pillow, his face looked more sallow and pinched than ever. The big, powerful man she had known had now shrunk considerably. The sight made her wince inwardly. He seemed so old, weak and vulnerable.

She sat beside the bed and placed the merest whisper of a kiss on his head. One hand touching him, she kept up her vigil for well over an hour but he showed no signs of coming out of his drugged sleep. At length she crossed to the telephone and dialled a number.

The voice at the other end was crisp and female.

'Can I help you?'

'Dr Gilmore, please.'

'Who is this?'

'His wife.'

'Oh. Hello, Mrs Gilmore. I'm afraid that your husband is out on a call at the moment.'

'I see.'

'Is there any message?'

'No. No message.'

'I'll tell him you called.'

'Thanks.'

'Goodbye, Mrs Gilmore . . .'

'Bye.'

Molly put the receiver down and went back to the bedside. She took her father's hand between her own. It felt cold and frail. She raised it lovingly to her cheek then replaced it gently on the bed. His breathing continued to come in short, grunting pants. She saw that he would never come out of the hospital alive.

The realization made her mind swim for an instant.

She had been desperately upset by her mother's death but that at least had been mercifully quick. This long, painful, protracted dying only served to increase the suffering. Molly's hopes were contradictory. She wanted her father to be spared any further pain and yet she could not bear to think of him dead. When he went, she would have nobody. Except Brian. And that was not the same. She knew that if her father passed away, an important part of herself would die as well. Molly shuddered. Having come to the hospital to bring comfort, she was now in need of it herself.

She went back to the telephone and dialled another number.

The restaurant was at South Street Seaport and it offered a superb view of the East River. It had a reputation as one of the oldest and best seafood establishments in the whole of New York and they were lucky to get a table at such short notice. Through the huge windows, they could see the gulls wheeling and dipping above the mouth of the river, and acting as unpaid convoys to any vessels that plied up and down. The Staten Island Ferry was breasting through the water towards them and a queue was waiting at the quayside. Moored below them were two square-rigged sailing ships in magnificent condition, museum pieces that were rich in legend.

Molly picked at her smelts with a fork.

'OK?' asked Frank.

'Yes.'

'Sure?'

'I'm fine.'

He enjoyed the view for a moment then turned back to her. She was still playing with her food and looking distraite. He was worried. Molly usually enjoyed their lunches together so much.

'What's the matter?'

'What?'

'You're thinking about something.'

'Am I?'

'Problems?'

She shrugged. 'I'm frightened.'

'Of what?'

'Everyt: ng.'

He chewed his own food and ruminated for a while.

'Did you go to the hospital?'

'Yes.'

'How was your father?' He saw her wince slightly and knew that his guess had been accurate. 'You don't have to say anything, if you don't want to, Molly.'

'You're good to me, Frank.'

'I try.'

'Tell me about New York.'

'Again?'

'Tell me. I like listening. Tell me some more, Frank.'

'You really are a glutton for punishment,' he commented with a lazy smile. 'Right. Where shall I begin? . . . In 1614, there were only four houses on the whole island of Manhattan. They weren't even houses. They were shelters for Dutch fur traders. All the way down at the tip of the island. The rest was swamps and marshes. Meadows. Hills. There was a whole system of little rivers and ponds. They had a real mosquito problem . . .' He broke off. 'Hey, this is boring.'

'No, it isn't.'

'I get started on this stuff, I never stop.'

'Then don't.'

'You serious?'

'If it gets boring, I'll tell you.'

'Alright, you asked for it . . . It wasn't until 1625 that the first permanent settlement was established here. The trading post was named New Amsterdam. The following year a man called Peter Minuit bought Manhattan from the Indians for the equivalent of twenty-four dollars. Say,

103

how do you like that? Twenty-four bucks! The check *here* is going to be more than that . . .'

He broke off as tears began to ru   down Molly's cheeks. Pulling out a handkerchief, he offered it to her but she refused it with a nod.

'Go on talking,' she pleaded, as the tears thickened. 'Please, Frank. I'm asking you. Go on talking . . .'

As soon as Brian Gilmore heard that his wife had tried to contact him, he rang the hospital and asked for the doctor in charge of John Trainer's case. Their exchange was succinct and couched in medical jargon. When Brian had found out all that he wanted to know, he asked the doctor not to mention to Molly that he had called. The man agreed at once. He understood the situation perfectly. And as a doctor, he thrived on keeping secrets. Without sparing his father-in-law a moment's sympathetic thought, Brian got on with his own work.

Frank Raftis squirmed in his seat as the meeting dragged on but he could not escape from it without showing extreme rudeness. He did his best to move things along and gasped his relief when the chairman finally declared the meeting over. He was out of the room and back to his office in a matter of seconds. The telephone rang. He snatched it up angrily, pressing the buzzer on the intercom with the other hand.

As Leona entered, he was virtually shouting at his caller.

'Yeah, yeah, I know that. I know that but nobody *else* seems to know that.' He punched something up on the computer screen. 'No, I'm just tired of saying the same thing over and over again!' Frank saw Leona. 'Did you get me a taxi?' he asked.

'Waiting downstairs.'

'Great.' He spoke into the receiver again. 'I'm looking at it right now. On the computer. It's right in front of me. What do you want me to *do*?' He rolled his eyes upwards then took a firmer line. 'Look Howard. I can't talk now. I'm sorry. I can't . . . No, I'm hanging up . . . No, I'm hanging up right now. I'm hanging up.'

He slammed the telephone down, grabbed his brief-case, nodded to Leona in passing and darted out of the room. The taxi was waiting directly outside and he dived into it without ceremony.

'Grand Central. And step on it!'

'In this traffic?'

'Please. Do your best.'

The journey was an agony of suspense as time began to run out. He had left himself only fifteen minutes to catch the train and the margin was a very slim one. Everything seemed to be against him. The traffic lights, the other vehicles, his own driver. When they were held up at another intersection, he leaped out of the car and poked money at the driver.

'But it's another two blocks,' argued the man.

'Quicker on foot . . .'

Frank ran as fast as the busy sidewalks would allow, dodging and swerving, praying that the train would some-how be delayed. When he reached the station, he raced across the concourse wildly and all but sent an old woman flying. His apology was yelled over his shoulder as he charged on through the gate and down to the platform, finding an extra spurt over this last stage. Then he stopped dead.

The train was just leaving. He had missed it.

In his tiredness and frustration, he leaned against a pillar for support and cursed his luck in getting the telephone call. It had robbed him of the one minute that

105

would have put him safely on to the train for his journey home with Molly. He was mortified.

'Frank?'

It was her voice. He turned to find her waiting for him further down the platform. Other commuters were streaming towards him but he barged straight past them until he got to her. Taking her by the arm, he led her off to a quiet corner of the platform and then threw his arms around her. Between kisses, the words rushed out.

'I love you, Molly . . .'

'Frank, wait . . .'

'I do . . . I do . . .'

'But you don't really . . .'

'I love you . . .'

Her protests were drowned beneath the fierce passion of his kisses and she held him as if she never wanted to let him go. She had waited for him. It said everything.

They caught the next train and rode between the cars so that they could be alone. They held hands, kissed, luxuriated in the simple pleasure of being together. Frank was ready to commit himself to her but doubts still gnawed away at the back of her mind. When the train pulled into Dobbs Ferry Station, those doubts were still there.

'Can I see you tomorrow?' he asked.

'Yes. No. I don't know.'

'I have to go in early. I'll meet you at one. Rizzoli's.'

'Frank . . .'

'Please.'

'I don't know.'

'Please.'

The train stopped. She nodded. He grinned.

Frank stood waving on the platform until he could no longer see her at the window, then he left the station and motioned a taxi over. On the drive back, he felt wonderful. Their relationship had finally blossomed. He had been able to tell Molly – and himself – that he loved her. Out of the trauma of missing the train had come this special moment for them.

He could not wait until the next day.

Ann was working in the garden when he got back. She had taken a keen interest in it over the past few months and there were many visible rewards for her efforts. Frank stood and watched her for several minutes before he let her know that he was home. Eventually, he called out to her.

'Hi.'

'Almost done. Dinner in thirty minutes.'

'No hurry.'

She went into the greenhouse and he sauntered down the path to join her. Ann wore rubber gardening gloves and was busying herself with a spray of some sort. She glanced up as he entered.

'Before I forget . . . I left the tickets on the hall table.'

'What tickets?'

'You're taking the boys to the Yankee game tomorrow.'

'Oh no.'

'What?'

'I can't.'

'Why not?' she asked.

'Well . . .' He thought about his arrangement with Molly.

'You forgot.'

'No, I didn't.'

'It went clean out of your mind,' she chided.

'I'm stuck all day with Vic Rawlins tomorrow.'

Ann smiled wearily. 'It's OK.'

'Damn.'

'It's OK. Really. I told the boys you might have to work. Don't worry about it. *I'll* take them.'

'I'm sorry, Ann.'

'No. I'd like to. I want to take them. I do. I was hoping it would work out like this.'

She gave him a smile of forgiveness but he did not respond at all. He was too busy brooding on the fact that he had just lied to his wife. About Molly. Indirectly. He had almost shocked himself.

'What's the matter?' she wondered.

'Lasky is getting a divorce,' he blurted out.

'Surprise, surprise.'

'He says he's not in love anymore.'

'Nobody is in love anymore. What else is new?'

'Were we in love?' he asked, seriously. 'Ever? I mean, were we ever in love?'

She found the question disturbing. 'Yes. I think so. But we were lucky. We survived it.'

He stared at her in silence. Ann reached for another smile to ease the situation, but a great dark cloud remained in her mind.

Molly Gilmore was still in the shower when her husband came out of the bathroom. He was wearing his suit and ready to go off to work.

'Hey!' he called.

'Yes. Be right out.'

'I'm leaving. When are you back?'

'Oh. I don't know.'

'How come?'

The shower was switched off. Molly emerged and grabbed a towel to wrap around herself. She pulled off her plastic shower cap and shook out her hair.

'How come?' repeated Brian.

'I have a lunch. And I want to do a few things. So.'

'Who with?'

There was a fractional pause. 'Oh. Isabelle. I'll call you.'

'Do that.' Brian remembered something. 'The drawings.'

'What about them?'

'Did you show her?' Molly nodded. 'Well?'

'She liked them. Isabelle's always liked my artwork.'

'That mean she offered you a job?'

'I'm not going back to work, Brian. Just yet.'

'Good,' he grunted.

'I'm only . . . keeping my hand in, that's all.'

'Ring me later.'

Without giving her his usual kiss, he went out. She heard him descending the stairs and put a hand to her face. She had just lied to Brian. For the first time in their marriage, she had told a deliberate lie about something very serious. Molly was torn between relief at having got away with it and sadness because of the wound which she had just inflicted on their marriage.

She began to dry herself on the towel. The day was an important one and it made her nervous and hesitant. When she had put on her underclothes, she searched carefully through her wardrobe for the right outfit to suit the occasion. She chose a green dress with a pleated skirt. As soon as she had put it on and seen herself in the mirror, however, she pulled it off again and flung it on to the bed. A beige suit was the next to be tried and that was discarded almost as quickly. Next came a pink blouse with a matching skirt but they failed miserably as well. Mild panic was now starting to set in. In her eagerness to try on the next dress, Molly put it on back to front and ended up with the label in her mouth. She shed yet another outfit and hurled it on to the bed.

She was now moving to and fro in front of her wardrobe like a caged tiger. She unhooked one hanger then replaced it, repeated the process with another hanger, then finally saw what she wanted. It was a loose fitting dress that was both smart and casual. Pale blue stripes ran down the cream-coloured material and she liked their effect in the mirror. Over the dress, she decided, she would wear a light coat with button-over pockets.

With the major decision taken, she now turned her attention to her make-up. She sat in front of the dressing table with a towel around her shoulders to protect her dress. Slowly, the make-up took shape. She widened an eye to apply a tiny amount of mascara and leaned forward to the mirror. She suddenly stopped, confronted herself, and took a deep breath.

'What are you doing? What *are* you doing?'

She sat there wondering for a long time.

Frank arrived at Rizzoli's Book Store a few minutes early. He was disappointed not to see her waiting and went inside to look for her. There was no sign of her anywhere and he came back out through the main entrance on Fifth Avenue. He stood there for several minutes and scanned the crowd for her face but she was nowhere to be seen. It had never occurred to him that she might not turn up at all but the longer he waited the more convinced he became that this was the case. He blamed himself. He had tried to rush her. And although he had declared his love for her, she had not been as willing to commit herself. His impatience had frightened her off. He had applied a little too much pressure and she had been unable to cope with it.

After one last despairing look up and down the avenue, he went back into the store. Molly had not come. It was all his fault.

And then he saw her.

She had come into the store through the entrance on 56th Street and was moving towards him between the book displays. He waved a wild hand and lurched forward to meet her. Their words overlapped in a mad jumble.

'Hi. I was waiting . . .' he began.

'Hello.'

'. . . at the other door.'

'I'm sorry. I'm late.'

'I didn't know . . .'

'I was . . .'

'. . . which entrance . . .'

'. . . late getting started. I got . . .'

'. . . so I came around . . .'

'. . . tied up . . .'

'Anyway.'

'So.'

'Here we are.'

'Yeah. Well.'

Customers were starting to look at them. They both spoke at once then laughed their apologies at each other.

'What?' she asked.

'Well. No. What were you . . .?'

'No, go ahead.'

'Oh.'

'Yeah.'

'Well . . .'

'It's OK. I was thinking the same thing.'

His heart thumped. 'You were?'

'I would have called you but . . .'

'Yeah. I know.'

'I just felt . . . I just felt . . .'

'Yeah,' interrupted Frank, conscious that they were in a very public place. 'What say we go somewhere else? Let's get out of here.'

'Right.'

'Hungry?'

'If you are.'

'I got just the place.'

The restaurant was located on a houseboat moored just

under Brooklyn Bridge and it provided its customers with a spectacular view of Manhattan. Passing craft tended to make the houseboat bob in the water but that only added to its charm. Frank complimented Molly on her appearance and made her glad that she had taken such trouble. She, in turn, told him how smart he looked in his open-necked shirt and light grey jacket.

Because they knew what had brought them there, they kept right off the subject and talked about anything and everything else. Molly volunteered more information about her career and admitted that she missed the excitement of the advertising world. Frank told her about the problems he was having on site and about the compromises they had had to make to erect the building within its budget.

They ate, they drank, they were in love.

The more they talked, however, the less they listened. As their mouths said one thing, their eyes were saying quite another. It was only a question of time before they found the courage to speak what was so obviously in both their minds.

Frank gave her another potted history of New York.

'. . . anyway, the city was Dutch then. And they were expecting an attack from the British in New England. So they decided to build a wall. But the bids from the private engineers were too high.'

'Never trust an engineer!' she said with a wink.

'Exactly!'

'So what did they do?'

'The city ordered the people to build it themselves and they did. From the East River straight across to the Hudson. That's why they call it Wall Street.'

'Did they attack?'

'Who?'

'The British.'

'Oh yeah. But they came from the sea. So the wall was useless.'

'You know so much, Frank.'

'Not really.'

'Tell me some more.'

'Maybe we've had enough, Molly . . .'

They had exhausted all the diversions. It was time to face up to the situation and take some action. Molly rubbed the palm of one hand with a finger then lifted her eyes to him.

'We're not very good at this, are we?'

He reached for her hand. 'Shall we go?'

'Where?'

'I have keys.'

Molly frowned. 'Keys?'

'It's an apartment,' he explained. 'A friend's apartment. I have keys.'

He took the keys from his pocket and put them on the table in front of her. Molly put out a hand to touch them lightly. Frank looked steadily at her and the bargain was sealed.

Then a strident voice cut in on them.

'Molly! Molly!'

With a young man at her heels, Isabelle was making her way through the tables towards them.

Chapter 8

Molly suddenly felt queasy but she had the presence of mind to close her hand over the keys. Frank jerked back at once and sat stiffly in his chair as Isabelle bore down on them. She came up to their table and gave Molly a knowing smile.

'Well, hi!'

'Isabelle. Hi. How are you?'

'Terrific. How are *you*?'

'Good. What are you doing here?'

'I'm trying to seduce this young man,' she giggled, pulling him forward for inspection. 'But I'm not getting very far, am I?'

Her escort could give her fifteen years. He was pure beefcake and had a flashy handsomeness that made for popularity among the ladies. He bared huge white teeth at Isabelle.

'I thought *I* was trying to seduce *you*.'

'Me and my big mouth!' said Isabelle, rocking slightly. 'You have to excuse us. We're a little stoned.'

'It's alright,' said Molly.

Isabelle now turned to Frank and beamed down at him.

'Hi. Isabelle.'

He shook her hand. 'Frank. Frank Raftis.'

'Have you met my friend, Molly?' she asked him. 'She's the nicest, sweetest person. The best friend I have. She's kind and considerate. And if anyone ever did anything to hurt her, I'd cut his balls off.'

The young man sniggered. Frank looked at Molly.

'Yes. We've met,' he announced.

'Don't let us keep you, Isabelle,' added Molly.

'Well, have a nice lunch,' said Isabelle, swaying. 'We're going. At least, I think we're going.'

'We're going,' confirmed her escort.

'Isn't he decisive?' she mocked.

'Bye,' muttered Molly.

'Right. Bye,' said Isabelle. 'See you around.'

'Yeah,' added Frank.

She pointed at him. 'Frank . . . Raftis . . .'

'Well remembered,' he said.

'We're going.'

The young man took Isabelle by the arm and led her back through the tables. They were soon leaving the restaurant altogether. Molly did not dare to look after her. She was still feeling horrified.

'Are you alright?'

'Yes,' she said. 'Sorry.'

'I don't mind.'

'I do.'

'Friend?'

'Yes. But the last person I wanted to see today.'

'These things happen.'

'Thanks.'

'For what?'

She handed him the keys that she had been holding.

'Let's go. Can we go?'

Frank summoned the waiter at once and paid the check.

The apartment was in a big, old brownstone house in Brooklyn Heights and the taxi dropped them right outside. They climbed the steps and Frank used one of the keys to let them in through the front door. A wide staircase confronted them and they went up it side by side. When they found the apartment on the second floor and went in, they were pleasantly surprised by the generous size and tasteful decoration. There was a subtle mixture of

115

old and new, some beautiful antiques living in harmony with the modern furniture. The ceilings were high with impressive mouldings and there were architraves round the doors. Old woodwork had been stripped and lovingly restored. The carpets had a faded grandeur. Garish paperbacks seemed at home in a dark oak bookcase. There was a trolley with drinks.

Afternoon light filtered through the window shutters and drew vivid pictures on the wall. It was quiet, peaceful, private. It was even romantic. The perfect place in which to begin an affair.

Molly moved tentatively around the room, pretending to examine various objects. Frank went over to the windows and opened one of the shutters. Light flooded in. They glanced at each other then looked away. She was timid, fearful, excited. He was shy, uncertain, considerate. It was the first time they had ever been alone together in a really private place and they were taking time to adjust to this fact. Again, it was the first time that they faced the reality of what was happening to them and that called for an even bigger adjustment.

Frank went over to her and took her hands. She found the strength to look up at him. They moved closer and their bodies touched, resting lightly against each other. There was electricity between them. Each little touch was an explosion of confused emotions. Finally, they came together in an embrace and tried to kiss away the agony of the months of waiting. The physical need on both sides was so powerful that it threatened to engulf them, yet it was tempered by a guilt and awkwardness that could only come from true innocence.

For both of them, it was in a sense the first time.

After the long opening embrace, Frank held her by the shoulders and turned her towards the bedroom. Molly led the way into a large, well-proportioned room with a double bed against one wall. The closed shutters had left the whole place in shadow and softened its lines. Molly went over to the bed, sat on the edge of it and undid a button on the front of her dress. Frank watched from the doorway as her fingers released another button and toyed with a third. He went slowly across to her and sat beside her.

Their hands touched again then they reached through each other's clothing, groping their way closer, feeling the intensity build inside them until it was almost unbearable. Frank eased her back on the bed and rolled on top of her, kissing, caressing, exploring, loving. Their limbs were tangled together in a frenzy of passion that went on and on until it demanded release. He grabbed at her clothes and tried to help them off.

But Molly stopped him.

At the very last moment, she changed her mind, froze, held him from her, then sat up on the edge of the bed again. She was shaking all over, gasping for air like a person who has just been saved from drowning. Frank lay quite still on the bed. Neither of them moved or spoke for a very long time. Then Molly whispered to him.

'I'm sorry.'

'Shhh . . .'

'I can't.'

'Shhh . . .'

'Sorry.'

'It doesn't matter . . .'

Both stayed exactly where they were, locked in a montage of memories, seeing themselves in the various situations that had led up to this ultimate meeting in a borrowed apartment. They saw themselves walking through the cheerful chaos of Chinatown, cycling together in Central Park, strolling along Canal Street, enjoying the sun in Union Square, visiting art galleries, sitting in restaurants, meeting under the clock in Grand Central Station. With a shared wistfulness, they saw each other for what they had been.

Two people in love with New York as their playground.

Molly began to straighten her clothes and do up her buttons. When she stood up, Frank reached across to her and wrapped his arms around her waist, burying his head between her breasts. She held him tightly and fought back the tears.

When they left the apartment and came out into the brilliant sunlight, he detained her on the steps. Pulling her very gently towards him, he kissed her softly on the lips. He spoke quietly.

'I love you.'

'I love you, too. But then what?'

'I know.'

'Once a week? Twice a week? Make arrangements. Tell lies. Go off into corners. For *what*? What would we have, Frank? What would that make us?'

But even as she spoke, Molly was drawing closer to him and the tender embrace became more desperate and urgent as their kisses almost obliterated what they were thinking and saying.

'The train is late! The train is late!'

'Don't shout like that, Mike.'

'No, here it is!' yelled Joe, pointing. 'Here it is!'

Both he and his brother jumped up and down on the platform until the train boomed past them then they raced towards Frank as soon as he emerged. He seemed taken aback by the fact that they had come to meet him but he caught Joe when the latter leapt up into his father's arms. Mike produced a baseball and displayed it proudly.

'Look Dad! I got this at the Yankee game.'

'Great,' said Frank, ruffling Mike's hair. 'Who won?'

'The Yankees, of course!'

'Best team in the world!' endorsed Joe.

Frank turned to his wife. 'How was it?'

'Fine,' she said, leaning forward to peck him on the cheek.

Over her shoulder, as the train drew away, he had a fleeting glimpse of Molly Gilmore sitting in the window. She gave him a pale smile as she was whisked out of his vision.

'Let's go,' decided Frank.

He carried Joe to the car and bundled him into the rear seat beside his brother. Ann drove. Frank kept seeing Molly's face.

'How was Vic Rawlins?'

'Who?'

'I thought you were with Vic Rawlins today.'

'Oh yeah. I was.'

'Lemme tell you about the game, Dad!' offered Mike.

'No, I will,' challenged his brother.

'*I* will,' insisted Mike, enforcing his seniority.

'Later, later,' Ann told them. 'Give your father a breather. He's had a long, hard day at work.'

'I have,' sighed Frank. 'He wants me to go to Houston.'

'Vic Rawlins?'

'Similar type of building. Consultant engineer.'

'Houston . . .' Ann sounded interested.

'I told him that it was out of the question,' said Frank, quickly. 'We're dug in here now. Besides, the offer wasn't big enough to tempt me.'

'You might have at least discussed it with me,' she complained.

'I *am* discussing it with you.'

'It was a fantastic game!' interrupted Mike.

'We had great seats,' added Joe.

'Boy, you should have seen that guy pitch!'

'Tell your father *later*,' ordered Ann.

'Now, Mom!'

'No, now, now!'

They took up the chant and bounced about on the rear seat.

'Stop doing that!' snapped Ann.

'You heard your mother,' said Frank.

He grabbed Joe and lifted him bodily over the back of his own seat so that he could pretend to spank him. Joe giggled happily. Mike immediately wanted to have his turn.

'Now me. Now me. Do it to *me*, Dad!'

The noise and laughter continued all the way home.

Molly Gilmore, by contrast, travelled in complete silence. The sight of Frank enjoying the welcome of his family had hurt her deeply, all the more so because Ann had been wearing a dress almost identical in colour to her own clothing. After the wonderful intimacy of the afternoon, Frank had been snatched away from her and she had been forcibly reminded that he belonged to somebody else.

She thought back over her day. It had begun with a lie to her husband and that still troubled her. Then the panic over what to wear. The botched meeting at Rizzoli's. Isabelle catching them out at the restaurant. The apartment. Her turmoil. Now this. It had all been too much for her and it sent her into a vortex of gloomy introspection. She was in love and yet she was unhappy. She wanted him and yet something held her back. He was hers and yet he had his own family. It all seemed so unfair.

During the ride home from the station, she continued to rake over the embers of the day. While the cab driver delivered an amiable monologue about the virtues of living in Westchester County, Molly was closing her hand over some keys and sitting on the edge of the bed in a strange apartment and watching a man being kissed by his wife at Dobbs Ferry. She could not understand why she had to pay for her pleasure with so much pain, why she was being torn in two by desire and restraint, why she felt at once guilty and liberated.

She was still caught up in conflicting emotions when the taxi finally arrived outside the house. She paid the driver almost absentmindedly then turned to walk up the stone path. Brian was waiting for her. Framed in the doorway, he looked sad, concerned and watchful.

Molly's first thought was that he had found out. Her heart pounded and she trembled all over. But there was no recrimination in Brian's manner as he walked slowly towards her and put his arms around her. She was bewildered.

'What? Brian? What is it?'

He said nothing but his grip tightened solicitously around her. Her mind was now racing through all the possibilities that could have made him behave like this.

'What's the matter? What is it? What? What? What?'

The Church bell tolled mournfully beneath an overcast sky. A full congregation attended the burial service for John Ambrose Trainer and many tears were shed into handkerchieves. For a man who had been so forceful and self-willed, he had a lot of friends and most of them seemed to have come to pay their last respects. As they sat in rows inside the church, they remembered him for his drive, his ambition, his dry wit, his outspokenness and his endearing selfishness.

He had been an important value in so many lives.

The operation which had been performed to ease his last days had in fact shortened them. Major surgery had sapped his already waning strength and his body had no powers of recovery. The doctor who had been in charge of his case was in the congregation alongside some senior members of the hospital administration.

Molly sat in the front row, her arm linked with Brian's, her hands scrunched up tight. She felt quite numb. The suddenness of her father's death had left her in a state of shock and she was still trying to come to terms with the news. For Molly Gilmore, it was not an isolated event. It was all part of one extraordinary day that veered between joy and despair and stopped at all the intermediate stages. Was his death a punishment? A judgement on her? Did she have to include that in the price?

Remorse brushed past her but could not get a hold. With almost cold detachment, she told herself that she should have been at the hospital when it happened. Having visited so regularly, it was ironic that he had died on one of the few days when she did not see him. Did her neglect contribute in any way? She accepted no blame. There would be time enough for that afterwards.

The coffin went past on a trolley that was guided gently along by the pall bearers. Brian nudged her and she stood up to lead the mourners down the aisle and out of the church. While the coffin was being eased into a hearse that was bedecked with wreaths and flowers, Molly looked blankly into the faces of the people who filed past her with muttered words of consolation.

'Molly. I'm so sorry.'

'Hello, Madge.' Her voice was toneless. 'Thank you.'

'Really.'

Brian spoke. 'Hello, Madge. How are you?'

'Oh, fine. Just surprised.'

'Well, we were expecting it,' he told her.

Next came a man. 'Anything we can do, Molly, just say.'

'No. Thanks, Bill. Thank you.'

Then another woman. 'Darling, are you alright?'

'Fine. You remember Brian?'

As more voices went past her, Molly just nodded.

'Sad day for all of us . . .'

'Hadn't realized that he was so . . .'

'Our thoughts are with you . . .'

'Your father was a wonderful man . . .'

'We'll miss him so much . . .'

'Just wanted you to know . . .'

'Did they say what . . .?'

'Your father . . .'

'Molly . . .'

Brian shielded her from any more comments and guided her towards the waiting car. She stepped in and sank back into the deep leather upholstery. Doors shut quietly as other vehicles filled up then the funeral procession began. The hearse pulled away soundlessly from the kerb with a long line of black cars behind it.

The sun had now broken through the clouds to redeem a dull morning. Everything suddenly had a bright and cheerful glow to it. Patches of blue were taking over the sky. Birds were singing. The air was warm and fresh. Hearse and cars shone brilliantly.

Molly sat in silence. Brian was calm but alert, watching his wife for signs of strain, waiting for the breakdown which had not yet happened, ready to cope, wanting to be in control. But Molly showed no sign of grief or strain. As they turned in through the cemetery gates after their long journey, she gazed out through the window.

'It's such a beautiful day, isn't it?' she said, easily. 'I don't think I can remember a more beautiful day.'

Brian did not answer. She smiled at him.

The cars stopped on a road some little distance from the grave itself and the mourners had to tread across the grass, picking their way between headstones and marble crosses. When everyone had gathered around the great brown slit in the earth, the burial service began. The priest was a tall, serious man with thinning hair and horn-rimmed spectacles. His sonorous voice rang out across the cemetery. More handkerchieves were needed as the coffin was lowered carefully into the ground. The priest intoned again.

'Forasmuch as it hath pleased Almighty God of his great mercy to take unto himself the soul of our departed brother here . . .'

Molly Gilmore felt the first searing pang.

'. . . we therefore commit his body to the ground . . .'

Her mouth went completely dry and she had difficulty breathing.

'. . . earth to earth, ashes to ashes, dust to dust . . .'

The full force now hit her and it made her reel. Her father was dead. She had been orphaned. There was no family left now. With all his faults and for all his awkwardness, she had loved him dearly and she now learned just how much he had meant to her. As she saw handfuls of earth being tossed on to the lid of the coffin, she felt a huge emptiness inside her, a sense of loss that made her begin to quake. He had gone forever.

And it was not just her father's death that she was mourning. Other things died with him, all of them bound up in that one fateful day when she had gone to an apartment in Brooklyn Heights with another man. Part of her marriage had died. Frank had died. Hope had died.

Everything she prized had been torn from her at once.

'Molly . . .' Brian saw that she was unwell.

'I'm alright,' she gasped.

But she clearly was not. Feeling sick and dizzy, she closed her eyes then opened them again and tried to focus. The mourners were a dull blur around the grave. The burial service was a faint echo in her ear. As she felt her knees give, she reached out to Brian.

'I've got you, Molly.'

'Bri . . . please . . .'

Her whole body was now shuddering. She was terrified that she was going either to faint or vomit. Muted sounds of fear and pain began to come out of her mouth.

'. . . no . . . I can't . . . take . . . Bri . . .'

'Come on,' he decided, leading her slowly away.

'I can't . . .'

'It's alright. Shhh. Alright.'

'He's . . . he's . . .'

'Molly . . .'

The tears came in a flood and the sobbing was totally out of control. By the time that he had got her back to the car, the noises of her grief sounded barely human. She was shaking and shrieking like an animal caught in a snare. Brian was having difficulty keeping her on her feet.

Behind them, at the graveside, the service continued.

'Come on, darling. I'll take you home . . .'

'Home?' Her eyes flashed.

He opened the car door. 'Home. Alright? We're going home, Molly. Right now. Come on . . .'

'I can't,' she said, resisting.

'It's alright,' he soothed.

'No!'

'Darling . . .?'

'I can't!' she yelled. 'Please!'

She tried to push him away but he held on to her. Molly become hysterical, struggling to get free, punching, biting, terrified of getting into the car. Brian grappled with her.

'Molly, stop! Stop it!'

'I can't!'

'What are you doing?'

'No!'

'Listen!'

'I can't!'

She redoubled her efforts to get away, clawing and kicking and screaming. It was all he could do to maintain his hold on her.

'For God's sake, Molly!'

'No, I can't! I can't! I can't! I can't!'

The violence and the screech came to a pitch and then suddenly cut out. Molly went limp and fainted into his arms. The other mourners were now staring in amazement at them. Brian lifted his wife and put her into the car. The funeral was over.

Frank Raftis waited on the platform with growing impatience and irritation. The train was a couple of minutes late and he was already cursing it. When it finally came into sight, he went to the end of the platform where the train itself would stop. As soon as it squealed to a halt, he dived into the open door of the first car and began the systematic search that he had been making every morning for several days now.

He went down the aisle of the first car, looking to left and right, making sure that he missed nobody out. Between the cars, he even checked to see if the bathroom was occupied then continued his patrol. The train was crowded and it took him some time to work his way through to the last car. As he was about to go in, the conductor came out and saw him.

'No seats in there, sir.'

'Yeah. I know.'

'Looking for someone?'

'Sort of.'

'That's different.'

The conductor went past him and began to clip the tickets in the next car. Frank tried to compose himself. This was his last chance. If Molly was not in the car, then she was not on the train. On the other hand, if she was in the car, she would not want to see him charging down the aisle wild-eyed and anxious. He made an effort to be as casual and relaxed as he could and strolled down the car, using the tops of the seats to keep his balance as the train rocked at high speed.

Molly was not there. Another morning without her.

Frank stood at the very end of the car and looked out through the window at the track fast disappearing behind them. He felt hurt and betrayed. She was deliberately avoiding him. What had he said to offend her? He ransacked his mind for memories of the last time they were together, riding home on the train together. He could recall nothing that had upset her, nothing that could make her drop him so completely like this.

Ann. It must have been Ann. Standing on the platform at Dobbs Ferry with the boys. He wished that Molly had not seen him with his family. That pale smile of hers was hiding a deep wound.

He tormented himself all the way to Manhattan and was still asking the same questions as he was buoyed up by the crowd in the main concourse. Not caring to have to speak to anyone, he decided to walk all the way to his office and set himself a brisk pace.

Leona gave him her usual cheerful welcome.

'Good morning, Mr Raftis!'

'Hi.'

'You're in demand today.'

'What?'

'Five calls already. Most of them urgent.'

'Put them on hold, Leona.'

'But . . .'

'I'm not taking calls this morning.'

'Mr Rawlins said it was vital that . . .'

'*Any* calls. Got it?'

Frank went into his office and shut the door.

127

'Yeah,' said Leona, ruefully. 'I got it.'

It was hopeless even trying to work. Frank simply sat at his desk and brooded. Time flew by. Leona was soon knocking on the door before bringing in his mid-morning cup of coffee.

'Thanks.' He summoned up a tired smile. 'And sorry.'

'That's alright, Mr Raftis.'

'It isn't alright. I shouldn't have snapped at you like that.'

'Bad night?'

'Something like that.'

'Hangover?'

'It'll pass . . .'

She went back to the door and paused. 'Oh, Mr Rawlins rang again. He said it was a matter of life and death.'

'He always says that. Keep stalling.'

'If you say so.'

'I do, Leona.'

She went out again and he sipped the coffee. It tasted bitter. He was soon brooding morosely again, testing out some of the other possible explanations. Her husband had found out. Or perhaps they had gone away together on holiday. Maybe Molly was ill. Or Brian was ill and she was staying at home to look after him. It was even conceivable that she had rushed off somewhere in response to a call for help from a friend or relative. But Frank always came back to the same thought. Why had she not contacted him? If any of those explanations were the right one, Molly would have rung him or written to him. Yet there had been no word.

It was almost as if she were dead.

Another hour flitted by as he tried to work it all out. Then the intercom buzzed and he flicked a switch before speaking into it.

'Yeah?'

128

'Sorry, Mr Raftis. You have a visitor.'

Hope stirred. 'Who is it?'

'Mr Rawlins. Says he won't go away till he's seen you.'

'OK' sighed Frank. 'Send him in.'

Vic Rawlins came storming in and accused Frank of hiding from him. He swept aside the apologies and came straight to the point.

'Houston, Frank. Yes or no?'

'Vic . . .'

'Stop messing me about, will you? There's plenty of other guys who'll jump at the chance. I need an answer. *Now*.'

Frank stroked his chin and pondered.

'*Now*!' emphasized Vic.

'Would you accept a provisional yes?'

Vic Rawlins burst out laughing. 'I just *knew* you'd come round in the end! This is great news, Frank. Congratulations.'

'Provisional, I said.'

'We both know what that means.'

'Yeah. Guess we do,' he admitted resignedly.

'What did it, Frank?' asked the architect.

'Did it?'

'Brought you round to the idea. You were dead against Houston when I first brought it up.' He chuckled and slapped Frank on the shoulder. 'Did you finally bow to my gifts of persuasion?'

'Not exactly.'

'Then what? Come on. You can tell me.'

Frank crossed to the window and stared out at Manhattan.

'Things have changed.'

He felt certain that they had changed forever.

Chapter 9

Isabelle was shocked and hurt when she saw her. Molly looked thin and frail. Her face was drained of colour and her eyes were dulled. She conjured up a brave smile when her friend first came into the bedroom but it soon faded. Even her beautiful hair seemed lifeless.

'Hello, Molly.'

'Hi.'

'How are you?'

'Getting better. Slowly.'

'Good.'

'Thanks for coming, Isabelle.'

'As if you could keep me away!'

'I needed to . . .' Molly glanced across at the bedroom door which had been left ajar. Isabelle got up and closed it before sitting down again. 'I needed to talk to someone.'

'It must have come as a terrible blow.'

'What?'

'Your father. I mean, from what I understood . . .'

'Maybe it's best this way,' said Molly, philosophically. 'He's been spared a lot of pain. And waiting.'

'Yeah.'

'The waiting is the worst.'

There was a lengthy pause then Isabelle took some fruit and a paperback book out of a plastic bag. She put them on the bed.

'The fruit is to make you well. The book is for when you're up to it. Spicey read.' She leaned in to whisper as Molly picked up the book and looked at the lurid cover.

'Don't let Brian see that. He wouldn't approve. Too much S.E.X.'

'Trust you, Isabelle!' said Molly with a tinny laugh.

'Never liked me, has he?'

'What?'

'Brian. I can tell. Whatever it is I do to all the other guys, I sure as hell don't do it to him!'

'No,' conceded Molly.

'So what has he got against me?'

'Nothing . . .'

'Come on. I can take it.' She grinned mischievously. 'I bet he says I'm a subversive influence on you.'

'And he's right!'

'Too true!'

There was a slight pause. 'He thinks you're trying to get me to go back to work.'

'I am. When can you start?'

'I can't start anything at the moment,' sighed Molly.

'Is it bad?'

'Terrible.'

'What are you on?'

'Some tablets Brian's given me.'

'Happy pills?'

'If they are, they're certainly not working.'

Isabelle took her hand. 'Guess I owe you an apology . . .'

'Why?'

'Last time.'

'Oh that.'

'Shouldn't have barged in on you like that.'

'You were bound to be curious.'

'Curious is one thing. I was plain nosey. And high on booze into the bargain! As for Mario . . .'

'Mario? Oh, your young man . . .'

'A passing fancy, believe me. Mario had his talents, I

suppose, but he was real dumb when it came to the social graces. It was wrong of me to jump on you with an ape like that in tow. Sorry.'

'Forget it.'

Isabelle gave her a slow smile. 'He was nice.'

'Thanks.'

'Kind of . . .'

'I know.'

'Have you . . .?'

'No.'

'So where is it at?'

Molly shrugged helplessly. She lay back against the pillows and tugged at her hair with a hand. Her breathing quickened. She looked at Isabelle for some moments as if trying to reach a decision and then began to unburden her soul.

'I think of him every day. Last thought before I go to sleep. First thought when I wake up. I talk to myself all day about him. Even when I talk to someone else, even while I'm talking to you now, I'm talking to myself about him.' She had twisted her hair into a little knot. 'Brian thinks I'm ill. He thinks that it has to do with my father. He thinks the stress and all, he thinks I might be having a breakdown. But I'm not, Isabelle. There's nothing wrong with me. Except that I love him.'

'Nothing wrong, she says!'

'Listen . . .'

'If you're in love, you're ill. Simple as that.'

'But it isn't!'

'Look, Molly . . .'

'I know you don't approve,' she countered. 'I don't approve either. No one should have to go through this. I agree with you. But that doesn't change it.' She became pensive and chewed at her lip. 'I suppose I should have slept with him. Maybe that would have made it easier. But

I don't think so. I think we were meant to be together. Even though we never will be. I think it's the right thing. No matter what it costs. You see? Everything else is wrong!'

Isabelle could not bear to see her in such distress. She put an arm around Molly and tried to soothe her. Molly cried silent tears and talked about him again. Isabelle listened. It was a help.

When it was time for her guest to leave, Molly begged her to come again soon. Isabelle promised that she would. Brian showed her out and she drove herself back towards the city, wondering how long Molly was going to remain like that. She had seen grief before but her friend's suffering was far more intense than any other she had known. She resolved to call again soon.

Brian, meanwhile, took Molly a warm drink and chatted to her. The bedside telephone rang and Molly flinched. He answered it.

'Hello? . . .'

The caller hung up without speaking. Brian put down the receiver.

'Who was that she asked?'

'Nobody.'

'It must have been somebody.'

'I think it was for you again.'

'Oh.'

'How many times is that now?'

'Listen, Bri . . .'

'No,' he said, firmly. 'I don't want to know about it. Thank you. I really don't want to know.'

Brian went out of the room and closed the door behind him. It was typical of him to walk away from a subject he found distasteful. It was the same with their child. He would not discuss what had happened. He had closed the door on that, too, in the mistaken belief that the problem would somehow go away.

133

Molly lay there in a quandary. She wanted to make contact with Frank and yet she was afraid to do so. She owed him an explanation but felt that speaking with him would only make her plight worse. In the end, she relied on instinct and grabbed for the telephone. When she dialled his number, however, she got an engaged tone. Her nerve failed. She replaced the receiver and buried herself deep in the pillows to cry again.

Frank Raftis tried to lose himself in his work and make up for weeks of neglect. He sat in front of his office computer for several hours, asking it to make calculations for him and noting down the results on a pad. Concentration on the bright screen eventually tired his eyes and he rubbed them with the backs of his hands. He checked his pad and was pleased with the amount of work he had covered. He was also grateful for something to engross him.

Rest brought his major anxieties surging back. He sighed, loosened his collar and sat back in his chair. As he looked at the computer, a thought elbowed him. He reached forward and tapped the keys with one hand.

The name MOLLY came up on the screen.

The computer soon printed out its response: WAIT! DISC DRIVE RUNNING.

He punched up the full name. MARY MARGARET GILMORE.

The same response. WAIT: DISC DRIVE RUNNING.

Frank now fed in one word: LOVE.

The response was predictable: NO DATA AVAILABLE.

It was a perfect summary of the last ten days or so. No data available. A complete lack of contact with her. Endless frustration. Bitter self-reproach. Recrimination. Disillusion. Anguish.

He swung round in his chair and snatched up the

telephone, dialling the number with sharp jabs of his finger. It rang out.

'Rawlins,' said the voice at the end of the line.

'Vic. It's me. Frank Raftis . . .'

'The very man. I've been going over the contracts.'

'Good. This call is by way of confirmation.'

'Houston, it is, eh?'

'Houston, it is!

There was nothing to keep him in New York now.

Ann Raftis sat alone at the kitchen table and helped herself to a glass of wine. The day had left her exhausted. After a morning doing household chores and an afternoon in the garden, she had taken the boys to the park then brought them home for a bath. Because they were in their usual energetic mood, bathtime was a physical struggle for her and she had to move from threats to sanctions and even on to a few well-judged slaps before she could get cooperation. By the time she finally got them both to bed, she was aching with fatigue.

But the drink was not merely to revive her. As she finished one glass and poured another, she realized that she was also trying to bolster her spirits. She was somehow frightened and the worst part of it was that she did not know what was causing her fear. It originated with Frank but that was as far as she could get.

Was she becoming afraid of her own husband?

She heard his car on the drive and hastily downed the drink, then she composed herself as best she could and resolved not to show her disquiet. A key was inserted into a lock and the front door opened then closed. His footsteps approached the kitchen. When he saw her there, he was surprised.

'Hey.'

'Hi.' She masked her worries behind a bright smile.

He kissed her lightly on the cheek and sat down.

'Sorry.'

'It's late, Frank.'

'I know.'

'You must be worn out.'

'Ready to drop.'

'I saved you some dinner,' she said, getting up and starting to set him a place at the table.

'Don't bother, Ann.'

'It's no trouble.'

'I can get something.'

'It's alright,' she assured him. This time her smile was a little too bright. 'It's nice to see you.' She took a plate of warm food from the oven and set it before him. 'There. Now eat that. I'll get you a glass.' She put a glass in front of him and filled it with wine. 'Nice?'

'Thanks.'

'Working late?'

'Calculations. I've been staring at that damn computer until I went dizzy. I hate that thing.'

'You always say it gets results.'

'So did Adolf Hitler.'

He looked down at the food then picked up a fork. After slicing a potato in two, he put half into his mouth and chewed. He nodded his approval to her. She was watching him closely.

'I talked to Vic Rawlins tonight.'

'Did you?'

'I told him yes about Houston.'

'Oh.' Her tone was non-committal.

'I figured it was too good a chance to miss.'

'But when we talked it over last time . . .'

'Yeah, yeah, I know. But I changed my mind.'

'I see.'

'Houston will be terrific,' he said with false enthusiasm.

'Are you sure about this, Frank?'

'That's why I rang Vic.'

Ann tried to get used to the idea but misgivings remained. The decision had been sprung on her before she had had the opportunity to go into all the implications. He had made the decision off his own bat. His lack of concern for her was one of the main things that was unsettling Ann so much.

'What does it mean?' she asked. 'When and all that?'

'September.'

'All of us?'

'That's the idea.'

'But what about the house?'

'We'll rent it out. They're throwing in a free house in Houston as part of the deal. I stuck out for that.'

'School?'

'They got plenty of schools in Houston.'

'You know how long it took Mike to settle. I'd rather hoped we wouldn't have to move him just yet. And Joe has taken to the school like a duck to . . .'

'The kids will soon get used to another school, Ann.'

Both of them felt the weight of the pause that followed. She poured some wine into her glass then sipped at it while he ate some more food. Ann worked up the courage to ask the question that had been troubling her ever since Houston had first been mentioned.

'Would you rather we didn't come?'

'What?'

'I mean, would you rather go alone?'

'No. No.'

'You sure?'

'No. That's the whole point.'

Another pause put more distance between them. Ann made a desperate effort to close the gap before it became impossibly wide.

'What's going on?' she demanded.

'Going on?'

'With us, I mean. What's the matter? What is it, Frank?'

'Nothing.'

'Is it me? Is it something I can do? Can I *do* anything? I mean, I'm not . . . Oh, Christ!'

'It's nothing.'

'No. Don't say nothing,' she retorted. 'Please. It's hard enough to ask. You can at least for Christ's sake answer me! You can at least lie! Make something up. I'm not an idiot, Frank. Don't tell me "nothing"!'

'Ann . . .'

'Alright. Never mind,' she said, dismissively. 'We'll go to Houston. Fine. Fine. We'll all go to Houston. I can hardly wait!'

Frank was moved by her plea. She deserved some kind of explanation from him. He sat there staring at his plate and groping for the words to tell her. When he spoke, his voice was flat and without any emotion. He raised his eyes to meet hers.

'I met a woman on the train. I . . . uh . . . don't know. Nothing happened. I mean, we didn't . . . we never . . . well. It's over now. Nothing happened. I'm not seeing her. I'm not having an affair. It's nothing like that.'

'No. It's worse. Isn't it?' She waited for a reply that did not come. 'I'm going to take a few weeks. I'll take Mike and Joe. We'll go to Denver, see my mother for a few weeks. Then we can meet in Houston.'

The longest pause of all ended. She stood in front of him and just stared down at him. Hurt and troubled by what she had said, Frank looked at her with concern. Suddenly, and with some force, she hit him across the face with her hand then stalked out of the kitchen. The slap had been more eloquent than any words she had used.

138

Frank sat there with his face stinging and his mind on fire. The food went cold on the plate and his wine was untouched. He stayed there long after he heard her feet moving in the bedroom above his head. When he finally stirred, he went quietly upstairs to the bathroom and filled the sink with cold water. Then he plunged his head in, came up for air, plunged again and held it there for a few long moments. He reached for a towel and dabbed at his face and hair.

He went to the master bedroom and inched the door open. The room was in darkness and Ann was asleep. He closed the door and tiptoed along the landing to the boy's room. Their door was ajar and he eased it open so that he could see inside. Both of them were fast asleep. Mike had the programme from the Yankee Game pinned on the wall above his bed. Joe cuddled a toy bear. Frank went right over to them and knelt down between the beds. He leaned over as if to kiss Joe but drew back guiltily, almost as if he had lost the right. He touched Mike's arm with his fingers then moved away.

He left the room as silently as he had entered it.

The night was dry and clear when he let himself out of the house. He got in the car, gunned the motor, reversed back on to the road then drove forward in the direction of the railroad tracks. When he came to the crossing, the long warning arms were vertical and so he was able to drive straight over. He felt the tracks under his wheels and was forcibly reminded of the significant part they had played in the whole business.

He turned the nose of the car towards Ardsley and accelerated. On the outskirts of the town, he pulled up under a lamp to consult his street guide. Finding the road he wanted, he set off again at a steady speed looking for his turnings.

The road in which Molly Gilmore lived was wide and

tree-lined. Her house was silhouetted against the sky. The porch light was on but the rest of the dwelling was in darkness. He slowed right down as he passed the house and looked up at it, wondering which room she was sleeping in at that moment. He felt at once marvellously close to her and hopelessly apart. It was the sort of house in which she belonged. It was exactly what he had expected.

Moving on past the house, he stopped the car at the end of the road and switched off the engine. His head dropped against the steering wheel. Slowly, and without any noise, he began to cry.

'Why not give it a whirl, Molly? What harm can it do?'

'No, Isabelle.'

'Part-time?'

'Not even that.'

'You're an under-used resource. Know that?'

'Yeah. You've told me so. Dozens of times.'

They were having a morning coffee together at Isabelle's office. Molly was so glad that she had made the effort to come into the city. She had still not recovered completely but felt that she had to make the effort to get out of Ardsley before it suffocated her. Isabelle, as always, was a tonic.

'Give me one good reason, Molly Gilmore.'

'I'm not ready.'

'How do you know?'

'Gut reaction.'

'Work means independence, honey. Don't you want that?'

'Yeah.'

'And dough?'

'Stop it, Isabelle,' she said.

'I see the dead hand of Doctor Brian Gilmore behind this.'

'You're wrong.'

'He *wants* you to go back to work?'

'No. But he did say he wouldn't stop me.'

'That was very noble of him!' sneered Isabelle. 'Makes it clear that he's opposed to the idea then dares you to go ahead with it.' She snorted. 'Husbands!'

'It's not like that.'

'Then what is it like?'

Molly hunched her shoulders. 'I'll tell you some day . . .'

Isabelle finished her coffee then reached for another biscuit. She was delighted that Molly was now well enough to get about and determined to help her all she could to get back on an even keel. Inevitably, her curiosity prompted her.

'Well?' She raised an eyebrow.

'No,' whispered Molly.

'Not heard from him at all?'

'Nor seen him. It's over, Isabelle.'

'That how you want it?'

'I don't have any choice,' admitted the other.

'In your position, I'd throw myself into my job.'

'You're not *in* my position. And besides, I don't have a job.'

'At the moment.'

Molly laughed. 'You never give up, do you?'

'Great to hear you laugh again.' She nibbled at the biscuit. 'Does Brian know?'

'Not really.'

'What's that supposed to mean?'

'He wouldn't listen.'

'Ah.'

'I tried to tell him but . . .'

'He didn't want to know. Ostrich technique. Bury your head in the ground.' She curled her lip in contempt. 'It doesn't work!'

141

'That's his way,' said Molly simply.

'If you want my opinion . . .'

'I know it already, Isabelle.'

'Sure!' said her friend briskly. 'Let's junk that subject and get back to the job offer.'

'Keep it on ice,' suggested Molly.

'Until when?'

'I'll let you know . . .'

She kissed Isabelle on the cheek and they exchanged farewells. Molly then came out into the street and wondered what she was going to do next. She had planned to go shopping then have a light lunch before returning home on an afternoon train, but Manhattan seemed to have other things lined up for her. Her legs started walking and she soon found herself turning a corner and heading for Rizzoli's. She stopped outside the main entrance and peered in the windows, trying to fight off the temptation to go in.

The pull was too strong for her and she was drawn into the store by an invisible magnet. Associations came rushing back. She walked on through to the section where they had first met and hovered near a display counter. New books had been set out attractively. Her eye sought the two volumes that had brought them together but neither was there. She searched the shelves in vain then asked an assistant for help. Molly was told that *The Big Book of Sailing* and *Gardening for All Seasons* were out of stock.

It was an apt commentary on her relationship with Frank.

She left Rizzoli's with a determination to carry on with her shopping but once again memory intervened. She was taken to cafes and restaurants that they had visited, to museums and art galleries, to markets and wharves, to Central Park. It was almost as if she were trying to persuade herself that it had all really happened. Molly felt the urge somehow to ratify her memories.

She stepped into another taxi.

'Brooklyn Heights.'

'Which part, lady?'

'I'm not sure.'

'That's a great help.'

'Just drive. I'll know when I get there.'

'I hope so, lady.'

'Just drive.'

They went over Brooklyn Bridge and into a maze of streets. She sent the driver first one way and then the other, craning her head through the window in the hope of seeing something familiar. But the search was fruitless. She had no street name, no number, just a vague sense of its location. Molly was shaken when they were unable to find it. An important part of her memories had disappeared and it weakened the whole structure. She lost her confidence.

'Take me to Grand Central,' she said.

'Grand Central!'

'Please.'

'That ain't in Brooklyn Heights,' he observed with sarcasm.

'I changed my mind.'

'Yeah.'

'Grand Central.'

When they reached the station, she paid him and hurried off across the concourse. Oblivious to the associations of the place, she caught the first train possible and did not relax until it began to pull away. She had escaped. It had been a mistake to go back into the city so soon. She needed more time to recover.

It was over. She told herself that she must accept that fact. What had happened between Molly Gilmore and

143

Frank Raftis belonged to the past. It was dead. Buried alongside her father in the cemetery. She looked at her watch and saw that it had just gone four o'clock. Where had her day vanished? No shopping. No lunch. Nothing. After coming into Manhattan in such buoyant spirits, she was leaving it in disarray. The tug of opposing emotions was almost destroying her.

The train streaked homewards and she started to feel better. Exhausted by her day, she dropped off to sleep for a few mi nutes and had a respite from the torment of her thoughts. She was much more in control of herself when the train pulled up at the station. Molly stepped out on to the platform and headed for the exit. The train started up and moved off. She suddenly stopped. It was not Ardsley.

Molly had got out at Dobbs Ferry Station.

Immediately she knew why and fresh hope was kindled. She went to the ticket office to get a train schedule then sat on a bench on the platform to consult it. Three trains per hour. He had to be on one of them. She crossed her legs, sat back and waited.

When the first train came in, only a handful of passengers got out and Frank was not among them. Molly told herself that it was too early for him and that he would not return for at least an hour, yet her pulse quickened as each new train came into view and she scanned the faces of everyone who alighted. No Frank Raftis.

The six twenty-five, Their train. He would be on that. When it finally pulled into the station, she got to her feet in anticipation and watched the doors of the train slide open. Over a dozen commuters alighted but there was no sign of Frank. He must have worked late at the office. Molly sat down again.

She lost count of the number of trains that arrived and then departed but it was sunset before she conceded that he was not coming. Molly had waited to no avail. It was another appropriate metaphor for their whole relationship. Waiting for something that never came. Wasting time. Burning up hope. Failing.

Molly walked slowly out of the station to find a taxi.

Chapter 10

It had been easy to hide it from the boys. They were not old enough to spot the signs. The prospect of extra time off school, the chance of seeing their grandmother and the excitement of air travel combined to blot out the true implications of the trip. But Frank and Ann Raftis could not conceal the truth from each other. As they stood with their children in the packed departure lounge at Kennedy Airport, they both knew that this was far more than a routine visit to Denver. It was a breathing space. An opportunity for each of them to take a long, hard look at their marriage. A period of examination.

'Ring me when you get to Denver,' he asked.

'Maybe.'

'I'd like to know you arrived safe.'

'Sure.'

Their flight was announced over the public address system and the boys immediately began to jump about.

'That's us!' shouted Mike. 'That's our plane!'

'Come on!' urged Joe.

'I want the seat by the window,' said his elder brother.

'No, I do!'

'*I* do!'

'It's not fair!'

'Hey, cool it, you two!' ordered their father.

'I'll sort them out,' said Ann.

'Why don't you . . . ?'

'Leave it to me, Frank. I'll cope.' She gave him a strange look. 'I'll have to, won't I?'

Frank knelt down and hugged his sons tightly.

146

'Now, you take care of your mother for me. OK?'

'Why can't you come with us, Dad?' wondered Joe.

'He's got work, stupid!' answered Mike.

'I'll see you both in Houston.'

'Great!' said Joe.

'Bye, Dad.'

'Bye, kids . . .'

He stood up and was about to kiss Ann when she stepped back a pace. She guided the two boys off in the direction of the departure gate.

'I'll be in touch,' she called.

'Yeah.' He pondered. 'Enjoy the trip!' he added.

The last sight he had of his sons was when their heads went bobbing through the departure gate. He missed them already and he missed his wife as well. He knew that his wife would be much further away from him than Denver.

He went out to the car park and began the long drive home. It gave him plenty of time to reflect on all that had taken place. He had lost so much over the past few weeks. His self-control. His sense of purpose. His appetite for his work. His enjoyment of his friends' company. His pleasure in life itself. His wife, maybe. Even his children. Certainly, his marriage could never be the same again.

Most of all, he had lost Molly Gilmore. What really tortured him was that he still did not understand why. He would accept it more easily if only he *knew*. But Molly would not speak to him or write to him or give him any kind of signal. She had flown out of his life for the time being. Just like Ann. Just like Mike and Joe.

Would any of them ever come back to him?

As he drove north up the Hudson River Valley, there were many sections where the road ran parallel with the railway tracks. More than once, a train sped past him and raked sadistically at his memories. He saw Molly walking

147

down the aisle between the seats, sitting in front of him, standing between the cars, nestling up against him, waving to him through the window as he got out. The train had been the central part of their world. It now served as a cruel reminder that that world had vanished.

Frank kept his eyes on the road ahead. It was time to put Molly Gilmore behind him. In the short term at least, his future lay in Houston. It would provide him with new horizons, new challenges, new friends. The work would come as a welcome bromide. He hoped.

He turned into his road with as sense of dread. When he had parked the car on the drive, he let himself into the house and stood in the middle of the living room. His home suddenly felt cold, empty and unwelcoming.

Frank realized that he was now completely alone.

Molly Gilmore sat in an armchair with a sketch pad on her lap and drew idly with a pencil. A couple of weeks in the house had made her restless and dissatisfied again and she began to wonder if it was time that she found herself a job. She weighed the advantages against the setbacks and found herself unable to reach a decision. Her pencil was still doodling when she heard Brian return. He came into the room and gave her a reflex smile.

'Hi.'

'Welcome home.'

'Nice day?'

'Nice enough.'

'Any calls?' he asked, his gaze watchful.

'No, Brian. None at all.'

'Good.' He took his bag into the study and came back again almost at once. 'Been out at all?'

'No.'

'Not even into the garden? Glorious weather.'

'I've just been sitting here quietly.'

'How long will dinner be?'

'Twenty minutes.'

'Fine.'

She began to draw again. 'Brian, I've been thinking . . .'

'What about?'

'Going back to work.'

'You?' His tone was discouraging.

'Only part-time. To see if I liked it.'

'But you don't *need* any job, Molly.'

'Maybe I do.'

'Why?' he argued. 'There's too much to keep you occupied here. And it's not as if you need the money. Apart from anything else, when they finally sort out your father's will . . .'

'Isabelle offered to fix me up.'

'You'd go and work in *Manhattan*?'

The question and its implications put an end to the discussion. Brian stroked at his beard and went off into the kitchen to pour himself a drink. Molly felt put down. When she looked at her sketch pad, she saw that she had drawn a train arriving at a station.

Thunder and lightning paid a visit to Westchester County and set the sky ablaze. Great rumbling noises were followed by vivid flashes of colour. Rain fell in sheets and drains slaked their thirst. The violence of the storm drove people indoors. Country lanes were awash.

The dramatic change in the weather affected the telephone lines. Callers had to contend with an interfering crackle. Frank Raftis was almost shouting into the mouthpiece.

'How's grandmom?'

'OK,' replied Mike, a faint voice in Denver.

'Uh-huh. Well, give her a hug from me.'

149

'A bug?'

'No, a hug, dummy. A *hug*!'

'A hug!' repeated Mike with a laugh.

'Yeah. Put your mother back on.'

'When will we see you, Dad?'

'In a few days.'

'Got lots to tell you. Joe and me went riding. On horses . . .'

'Save the news till we meet up, Mike.'

'OK. Bye, Dad . . .'

'Bye.' He waited for Ann to pick up the receiver. 'Hi.'

'Hello, Frank.' Still that same neutral voice.

'I'm all packed. Just hanging on for the car.'

'Taxi?'

'No, they're sending a limo.'

'That's nice.'

'Yeah. Shows they really want me.'

'Have you locked everything up?'

'Yeah.'

'Switched everything off?'

'Of course. Don't worry.'

'Was there any food left in the . . .'

'I can handle it, Ann. Alright? The house is fine.'

'Did you get that list of things to bring? Mike needs his roller skates and Joe's been lost without his baseball bat. Then there's the . . .'

'I told you,' he interrupted. 'Everything's taken care of. I got half the house packed in these damn suitcases. Don't worry. It's all here.' There was a pause. 'I missed you, Ann.'

She chose not to hear him. 'Must go. Mom wants me.'

'I'll call from Houston.'

'Yeah.'

'As soon as my plane lands.'

'Check the house again before you leave.'

150

'I will.'

'Carefully, Frank.'

'I will, I promise.'

'Good.'

'Bye, then.'

'Bye.'

'Oh, listen, Ann. I just remembered . . .'

But he was too late. She had hung up. Outside the window, the lightning was at its most spectacular. Rain drummed on the panes. Frank glanced out inho the turbulent night then recalled his promise. He made a final tour of the house to make sure that all doors and windows were locked and all lights switched off. There was still some time before his chauffeur was due to arrive and he decided to have a snack. The choice was less than exciting. The refrigerator was quite empty and all the cupboards yielded were some crackers and a tin of tuna fish.

He got himself a plate and a fork, opened the tin then took the meal through to the living room. As he began to spread the fish on to a cracker, he thought about all that he was leaving behind in Dobbs Ferry. His sadness and regret haunted him afresh.

He forgot all about the snack and brooded on his predicament. Then he got up and reached for the telephone.

Molly Gilmore was running a bath for herself when the telephone rang. She was wearing a bathrobe and slippers and was about to slip them off to get into the water. She tested the temperature with her hand. Then she became aware that the telephone was still ringing.

'Brian! Brian! Telephone!'

When the instrument continued to ring, she turned off the taps, went through the bedroom and opened the door to shout down the stairs.

'Brian? I'm sure it's for you? Bri?'

There was no answer. She let out a sigh and crossed to the telephone. As soon as she picked up the receiver, she realized that she was a second too late. Whoever was calling had just hung up. She put the receiver down and went back into the bathroom. The rain was now lashing the windows and more thunder was reverberating. She pulled the plastic curtains shut and kicked off her slippers. As she was removing her bathrobe, the telephone rang again. Molly clicked her tongue in irritation and pulled the garment on again. The ringing tone seemed to be more strident this time.

She snatched up the receiver and spoke into it.

'Yes. Hello. Hello? Hello? Who is . . . ?'

Her voice died on her lips. There was no sound from the other end of the line but she knew at once who was calling her. She was fixed to the spot, not daring to speak. The telephone burned in her grasp. With one hand, she pulled the bathrobe more tightly around her.

After a lengthy pause, Frank's voice spoke.

'Hi. It's me.'

'Yes.' She gulped for air. 'Hi.'

'I'm sorry. Are you . . . uh . . .'

'What?'

'Are you in the middle of something?'

'No. A bath. I was going to take a bath.'

'Oh.'

'Yes.'

She heard him clear his throat. 'Are you alone?'

'Sort of.'

'So am I.'

'Where are you?' she sounded concerned.

'At home.'

'Are you alright? Is anything wrong?'

'Yes. I miss you.'

The smile began on her face and spread right through her.

'Do you?'

'Yes.'

'Well. I miss you, too.'

There was another pause while he cleared his throat again.

'I'm leaving town. I'm going to Houston.'

'That job?' She was surprised and hurt.

'I decided to take it. I'm leaving tonight. Now. Pretty soon. Just waiting for the car . . .'

She felt despondent. 'How long are you going for?'

'Eight, nine months. Maybe a year.'

'A year!' It seemed like an eternity.

'I figured it was time to make a break,' he said, with forced confidence. 'How have you been?'

'Terrible.'

'That so?'

'My father died. And I missed you. I've been through hell.'

'Oh.'

'I feel terrible, Frank.'

'Yeah. Listen. Christ, why do people always say "listen" on the telephone! It's crazy . . . Molly, what else are you doing?'

'Doing?'

'Apart from the bath.'

'Nothing? What?'

'I want to see you. Can I see you? Before I go? I'm sorry. I know I, I've only got a few minutes. I don't want to go.'

'Frank . . .'

'I don't want to do anything, Molly. I keep turning off lights. Please. could I see you?'

'Well . . .'

153

'Could I just *see* you? That's all.'

'I don't know . . .'

'*Please*.'

Before she could answer, Brian came into the bedroom.

'Oh. You did get it,' he said.

She covered the mouthpiece with a hand. 'Yes. I got it, Brian. It was for me.'

'Who?'

'Isabelle. She wanted a chat.'

Brian went on into the bathroom and began to run water into the sink. He left the door ajar and Molly was terrified to speak. At the other end of the line, Frank was trying to account for the long silence. His voice took on new urgency.

'Is somebody there? Can you talk? . . . Look, just . . . Could you come here? Just . . . I'm on Havenhurst, just below Main. Please, Molly. I'll wait for you.'

At that moment, Brian came out of the bathroom and stood beside her, his suspicions aroused by the fact that she was saying nothing to her caller. Molly froze, not knowing what to do. Brian watched her steadily. He knew who was on the line.

'Molly! Are you there?' Frank again. 'Say something.'

'Well, thanks for calling,' she said, quickly. 'And have a good trip. Call me. Call me when you get back. OK?'

She put the receiver down before he could reply.

'Trip?' said Brian. 'Where?'

'Oh, off with one of her young men somewhere.'

'Isabelle, that is?'

'Yeah, yeah. Isabelle.'

They both knew that she was lying. She shrugged, pointed towards the bathroom then edged over to it.

'My bath will be getting cold.'

'Yeah.'

The telephone rang again. Brian saw her start.

154

'You want to answer it?' he asked.

'No.'

'You want *me* to answer it.'

'No.'

'Are you sure?'

'No. Please.'

They both waited as the telephone rang out for several minutes with unwearying persistence. Outside in the night, the storm still raged at its fiercest. The telephone provided a descant to the tumult.

Eventually, it stopped. Brian was grimly satisfied.

'Well. That's that. I could use a drink. Would you like a drink?'

'I don't know.'

'I'll fix us a drink,' he said and went out of the room.

Molly stood there hypnotized by the telephone. Should she ring him back? Ignore his plea? Try to wipe out all that had happened between them? In a flash, the answer came to her. She knew exactly what she had to do.

Flinging off her bathrobe, she grabbed her underclothes and put them on as fast as she could, then she clambered into a dress and stepped into a pair of shoes. She was still doing up the dress as she came hurrying down the stairs.

Brian was fixing the drinks in the living room when Molly burst in. She was pulling on a raincoat. He was taken aback.

'Where are you going?'

'To see him.'

'Molly . . .'

'He's going away, Brian. I won't be long. I'm just going to see him. I'm just going to say goodbye.'

'I don't think that's such a good idea.'

'Brian, please . . .'

'Look, I don't mind,' he said, evenly. 'It happens to everybody, this kind of thing. It's not unusual. In fact, it's pretty common. Isn't it? In this day and age. I understand that.' He took a step towards her. 'But enough is enough. Don't you think? If he's going away, then that's the end of it. Isn't it?'

She studied his face for a few seconds then decided.

'I'll be back.'

'I'll be here.'

Molly went rushing to the front door and dashed out in the rain. With a drink in his hand, Brian went out the porch and watched her start the car, back it into the road, then accelerate fiercely away, sendiing up a wave of spray in her wake. When the rear lights disappeared around the corner, he went back into the living room.

There was a wry smile on his face as he walked across to the telephone and stroked it idly with his finger. He shook his head. Then he swallowed his drink in one gulp.

Frank Raftis threw the uneaten tin of tuna fish into the bin and hurled the crackers at it. His last hopes had been dashed. Having finally made contact with her after so many vain attempts, his spirits had lifted. Molly Gilmore had not walked out on him. She, too, had been suffering. She, too, had become acquainted with despair. And she had admitted that she missed him. That had stirred him most of all.

Suddenly, it was gone. She had hung up on him and put a decisive end to it all. There was no point in waiting for her now. She would not be coming. Ever.

Car tyres hissed on the drive and he went to the door. His chauffeur got out and scurried across to the porch. He wore a cap and his raincoat collar was turned up.

'You sure picked one hell of a night, mister.'

'I know,' agreed Frank.

'Bags?'

'The cases are right here.' He indicated them standing

in the hallway. 'These go. All of them. I'm going to lock everything up.'

'Sure.'

While Frank made another unnecessary tour of the house, his chauffeur loaded the suitcases into the boot of the limousine. The man then came back to shelter in the porch, grimacing as the sky was lit by another firework display of lightning. Frank came back downstairs, turning off switches behind him, taking his time, feeling the urge to linger. The driver was more anxious to leave.

'All set?'

'Yeah. I guess so.'

'We'd better get moving,' suggested the man. 'This weather, the airport's going to be a mess.'

Frank hesitated. 'You go on. I have one more thing.'

'Make it snappy.'

While the man went to get into the car, Frank picked up the telephone in the living room once more. He dialled the number that he had dialled so many times in recent weeks. It rang out. Eventually, the receiver was picked up at the other end of the line.

'Hello?' It was Brian's voice.

'Hello. I'm . . . uh . . . Is Molly there? Molly Gilmore, could I speak to her, please?'

'Who is this?'

'Uh . . . a friend.'

'I'm sorry,' lied Brian. 'She's . . . gone to bed.'

'Oh.'

'I'm sure she's asleep now. Can I take a message? I'm her husband.'

Frank's heart sank. 'No. No message. Thank you.'

'Shall I say who called?'

There was a click as Frank hung up. Molly had gone to bed. That was her response to his plea. She did not want to see him.

157

Frank switched off the lights and went quickly out.

The storm was at its peak as Molly Gilmore drove wildly along the road to Dobbs Ferry. Rain pounded her windscreen and the wipers swished away at maximum speed to give her some visibility. Slippery wet roads were another problem and she was dazzled from time to time by the headlights of oncoming vehicles which set alight the shining pools of water all around her. She was travelling at a breakneck speed that would have been risky in the best weather conditions. During a thunderstorm at night, it was almost suicidal.

What kept Molly going was the consuming need to see him before he went away. The tone of his voice had told her everything. He had been through torments. The least that she could do was to answer his plea and spend a last few minutes with him. It was not the ideal way to bring it all to an end but it was far better than letting him drift out of her life, feeling bitter and wounded.

The curve of a bend deceived her for a second and she had to brake to reduce speed. Her tyres squished violently on the sodden surface of the road and there was the beginning of a skid, but she swung the steering wheel over and corrected it. As her way seemed to straighten out again, she jabbed her foot down viciously on the gas pedal. Every second was vital.

Ardsley to Dobbs Ferry. Her last journey in a relationship that was composed almost entirely of journeys. They had fallen in love in transit. They had celebrated by making endless visits to various parts of the city, by touring New York with their shared happiness. A love affair on the move.

Thunder boomed in the distance and forked lightning cut a great jagged piece out of the black sky. In the split second of illumination, she thought she saw something over to her right, something heading in the same direction, a long streak of light. As she got closer, she realized what it was. A train. Speeding through the deluge. The Metro North Commuter Railroad. Yet again.

She remembered the railroad crossing up ahead and knew that it was essential for her to get there first. To have to wait for the train to shoot past would be to waste valuable time. The needle on her speedometer swung crazily over as she called for maximum power from the engine. She could see the train more clearly now and hear its metallic clatter as it hurled itself along the track. Car versus train. Molly Gilmore against time itself. The crossing leapt up out of the gloom ahead and she gritted her teeth for one last effort, desperately hoping that she would make it, praying that she would reach Frank before he left.

But even as she approached, the warning bell was clanging, the red light was flashing and the vertical arms were descending across either side of the crossing. Molly thought for an instant that she would just get through before the arms were horizontal but she saw with horror that she would not. Her foot hit the brake as hard as it could and sent the car into a terrifying skid. She was certain that she was going to end up under the train itself as it came zooming up, but the car instead swung sideways at the last moment and stopped with a screech of pain inches from the warning arm.

Molly watched in sheer panic as the train careered past within feet of her, its lights flashing across her white face. She covered her ears against the noise and closed her eyes against the blinding light. The car shook and vibrated as if it was going to fall to pieces. The train seemed endless. As its clamour reached its peak, she cowered away from its menace.

All at once, it was gone, carrying its awesome power

into the night. She was badly shaken but not seriously hurt. Something told her, however, that she was now too late. The affair was over. She would never be in time for him now. The train which had brought them together in the first place had severed them unmercifully.

She waited until she had collected herself, then switched on the ignition. The engine protested. She tried again and the engine turned lazily then gave out. Molly was stranded. Though she kept turning the ignition key, she knew that it was to no purpose. The car was yet another casualty of the train's remorseless might. It had been tossed aside for daring to think it could match the train for speed. Molly gave up.

Slowly and with great care, she got out of the car. She was drenched within seconds but the rain felt good and ashe lifted her face up to meet it. When she looked around, there was nothing in sight. The arms were vertical again and the way to Dobbs Ferry was clear but she had no means of getting there. She turned around and started to walk away from the crossing.

Towards home.

Chapter 11

Christmas blessed New York City with its traditional cheer and its untold opportunities for commercial exploitation. Decorations enlivened the eye, Santa Claus was back on every corner, and the brass bands worked through their repertoire of carols. An already crowded metropolis threatened to choke itself with people. Traffic jams were the norm. Cab drivers displayed frayed nerves. Naked panic reigned in many stores as last-minute shoppers fought for service. It was all very predictable, familiar and seasonal.

Snow had been forecast by the weather experts but only a few tiny flakes consented to fall and hopes of a White Christmas were thwarted. New Yorkers jostled their way along the busy sidewalks with a mixture of frenzy and goodwill. Children were dragged open-mouthed past windows full of toys. Parents consulted lists and put a price on Christmas happiness. Tradesmen prospered. Cops complained.

Laden with parcels and packages of every size, Molly Gilmore moved slowly along Fifth Avenue with a thick coat and a frown of consternation. Christmas would not be the same for her this year, less a time of celebration than one of commiseration. As she looked down the avenue towards Central Park, she felt a pang as she recalled her father's death. This time last year he had partaken of Christmas as a privileged observer in his luxury apartment. She missed him and his panoramic view of the park.

Molly strode on past a store whose windows were a

series of glittering snow scenes. Above her head, a series of red flags offered Christmas greetings in a variety of languages to a cosmopolitan city. Molly glanced up and sighed. It would not be a Merry Christmas for her in any language. Just a lonely one.

She walked on past St Patrick's Cathedral, maintaining its dignity amid the accumulated chaos, offering a sculptured serenity to a populace deafened by noise. On the next corner, Molly saw a Sabrette hot dog trolley with steam rising from it. She went past it, stopped, considered, then turned around to go back.

'Hot dog. Just mustard.'

'Nothing else?'

'Just mustard.'

'You got it.'

She ate as she walked, her purchases under her arms or in her other hand. The hot dog tasted as it should on a cold Christmas Eve. It revived her for a further assault on the stores.

Rockefeller Plaza, meanwhile, was offering its usual range of delights to a large, promenading audience. A Salvation Army Band was booming its way through *Silent Night* and an uniformed girl was taking a collecting box around. The skating rink was full as young and old alike glided around the ice in search of fun. Flags of many nations fluttered above them. The nearby Prometheus Fountain sent water up in everlasting spirals of joy.

Frank Raftis watched the scene with casual interest. Over to his left, the choir was attacking *The Holly and the Ivy* with more gusto than harmony and he moved a dozen paces or so in order to come within range of the band instead. He carried a few bags but nowhere near as many as on the previous Christmas Eve. His face was lined and serious and there was a cynical line to his mouth. He took a last disenchanted look around the plaza then turned away.

Five minutes later, he walked into a restaurant.

'Hey! Frank!' Ed Lasky saw him first.

'Hi, Ed.'

'Welcome home!'

'Thanks.' Frank dumped his bags down and took a seat.

'You looked bushed.'

'I am.'

'Working too hard?'

'Partly that . . . How are you, Ed?'

'Great. I'm great. Well, I'm OK. I'm good. Yeah, I'm fine.' He reached for a bottle of champagne on the ice bucket and poured out two glasses. 'I thought we'd make this a tradition. You know, every Christmas Eve we could meet for a drink.'

Frank was impressed. 'What's this? Champagne? What are we celebrating?'

'I'm getting married,' announced Ed.

'What?' Frank laughed. 'When?'

'June.'

'To Carol?'

'She finally bullied me into it.'

'And Susan?'

'The divorce hasn't come through yet but it's only a question of time.' He chuckled cynically. 'Out of one noose and into another.'

'I hope it'll work out for you, Ed,' said Frank, seriously.

'Thanks. How's Ann? The kids?'

'Well, fine. They're in Denver.'

'For Christmas!' He was surprised.

'For good. We're separated.'

'What!' he exclaimed in disbelief.

'Separated.'

'Oh, shit.'

Frank looked around the restaurant. 'We shouldn't come to this place, Ed. I think it's bad luck.'

'Oh, Frank. No. No . . .'

Frank raised his glass in a toast. 'Merry Christmas.'

The toast had a sardonic ring but they drank to it. Ed's face was clouded with concern as he leaned forward.

'What happened?'

'Long story.'

'I got all the time in the world, pal.'

'Never mind, Ed. It's not important.'

'What do you mean "never mind"? You can't be separated.'

'Why not?'

'Because you're my pal. My hope.'

'What are you talking about?'

'Whenever anybody dumps on marriage, I always say I know a marriage that worked. I know a marriage that's going to last. Frank Raftis.' He looked balefully at his friend. 'Jesus.'

'People change, Ed. Everything changes.'

'Yeah. Sure. But what happened?'

Over the meal, Frank told him. The move to Houston had been a disaster. The job had been uncongenial, the children had been unhappy at their school, and Ann had found herself unable to forgive and forget. Instead of running away from his problems, Frank had simply transplanted them to Texas. Under so many pressures, the marriage had weakened.

'I spent three months in Houston walking into walls, Ed. I didn't know where I was. All I could think about was Molly Gilmore.'

'Call her.'

'No.'

'Pick up a phone and call her,' urged Ed.

Frank shook his head. 'It's over. She wouldn't even give me five minutes to say goodbye. I don't want to talk to her. I don't even want to see her again.'

164

'Then what *do* you want?'

Frank emptied his glass of the last of the champagne.

'I want her back.'

'Come to Barbados with us.'

'No.'

'Come on, Molly.'

'I can't.'

'Why not? I'm sure he has a friend,' argued Isabelle. 'These guys always have friends. They lift weights together.'

'I don't like the idea of Christmas in hot weather. Sunshine. Beaches. It makes me nervous.'

'You're a free woman now, remember. It's time you started behaving like one.'

'I'm a slow learner.'

They were walking alone the sidewalk together after lunching at a restaurant. Isabelle was taking it upon herself to organize her friend's Christmas for her and Molly was resisting. She was not ready to pursue the good life as strenuously as her friend did.

Isabelle returned to the attack.

'What are you going to do? Sit home in that big house all alone and sing Christmas carols?'

'Probably.'

'Come to Barbados . . .'

'Isabelle . . .'

'Sun, sea and sex. Can you think of a better combination?'

'How about happiness and love?'

Isabelle gave a harsh laugh. 'Don't get me started, honey!'

They strolled on until they reached the office building where she worked and stepped into the doorway. Isabelle indicated the bags and parcels that Molly was carrying.

'Why so much stuff when you've got no one to buy for?'

'It's all for me. I need cheering up.'

'Don't we all?' sighed the other.

'You have your way. I have mine. Enjoy Barbados.'

Isabelle's face hardened. 'This may sound dumb but I've got half a mind to stay at home with your instead.'

'Why?'

'The truth is, you know, I don't think I like men anymore.'

Molly kissed her. 'Have a nice time.'

'I'm going to ring you up every day and bug you until you take that job. Be warned.'

'I will. Oh, don't forget to send me a postcard.'

'I'll do better than that, Molly. I'm going to take pornographic pictures. And I'm going to make you look at them!'

She gave a farewell laugh and went into the building. Molly looked lost. In the middle of a crowded sidewalk, she was all alone.

Frank Raftis ended a dispiriting day in the city by walking around to Rizzoli's Bookstore. He was entitled to indulge himself in a few memories to warm up what was otherwise going to be a fairly bleak Christmas. As he went in through the main entrance, he reflected on the difference that a year had made to his life. Last Christmas he was rushing madly around buying for his wife and children. This year he was simply going through the motions, impelled by some urge to try to lose his misery in the Christmas spirit of the city.

Rizzoli's was thronged. He moved through the various sections, glancing at books and prints, having no intention of buying anything. Suddenly, he was confronted with a book that he recognized. It was a copy of *Gardening For All Seasons* and it was on a table marked 'Christmas

Bargains'. The book was back in stock. He picked it up and leafed through it. A familiar voice spoke.

'I can recommend it. I had a copy last Christmas.'

He raised his head to see Molly Gilmore smiling at him from the other side of the table. She looked radiant. Frank was thrown into a state of confusion and embarrassment. His first impulse was to reach out and take her in his arms but he was convinced that she had deliberately put an end to their affair and would not welcome such a show of affection. It was ironic. She had been continually in his thoughts for months yet now she was actually in front of him, he was completely disconcerted.

She saw his unease and broke the silence.

'Hi.'

'Hello. You surprised me.'

'Sorry.'

'No. Good. I mean, it's OK. So. How are you?' He went around the table to her. 'You look great.'

'I'm fine. How are *you*?' She gestured at him. 'You're back.'

'Yeah. Last week. It was good to get home.'

'Just in time for Christmas.'

'Yeah. Christmas. Right. Yeah.'

It was her turn to feel uneasy. She took a deep breath.

'I'm glad I ran into you. Uh. I've wanted to tell you, explain. That night you called, the night you left . . .'

'Oh. Well . . .'

'I wanted to explain what happened.'

'Oh. That's OK.'

'No, really . . .'

'It's OK. You did the right thing,' he told her.

'No, I didn't . . . I mean . . .'

'Yeah. I understood. It was a bad time for me. That's all.'

'Oh. Yeah. Me, too.'

167

'Really?'

'Yeah.'

People were milling all around them. It was hardly the best place to hold such a private conversation but neither of them had the presence of mind to suggest going someone else. Each of them felt at fault. They lacked confidence.

'I should never have called you that night,' he apologized with a shrug. 'I'm sorry.'

'Don't be sorry.'

'Well . . . I don't know what I expected to happen. I guess I was a little confused.'

'Frank . . . listen . . .'

'It's OK. I think we were *both* a little confused.'

'I don't know. I guess so.'

'Yeah.' He rose to a smile. 'You look . . . you look terrific.'

His gaze unsettled her. She wanted to explain to him but could not find the words to do it. She just stood there tongue-tied for well over a minute. When she finally spoke, the question was blurted out.

'How's the family?'

'Oh. Fine. Great. Yeah.'

'Mike and Joe?'

'Growing.'

'They would be.'

'Yeah. You know. Kids are amazing.'

'Yes,' she agreed. 'Hope.'

Puzzled at first, he then remembered a snatch of conversation they had had a long time ago. He nodded sagely.

'Oh. Right. Hope.'

'You can't live without it . . .'

Another long wait as they searched each other's faces.

He spoke quietly. 'And . . . uh . . . how's, how is . . . uh . . . ?'

'Oh, good. We're uh . . .' She wanted to tell him the truth about Brian but it would not come out. 'We've been . . . well, he's fine.'

'Good. Well.'

'Yeah.'

'I better get moving.'

'Yeah.' She looked at his bags, 'Not so much to carry this year.'

'No.'

'Listen . . .'

'Yeah?'

'Call me. We'll have lunch. Something.'

'Oh. Great.' His tone was polite rather than enthusiastic. 'Yeah. I will. Yeah.'

She offered her hand and he shook it. The contact was electric for both of them as they touched once again.

'Take care of yourself,' she said.

'I will. You, too.'

'Merry Christmas.'

She left him a last smile and walked towards the exit. He went quickly after her and caught up with her by the door.

'Molly?'

When she turned, they were face to face. He put his arms around her very gently. He wanted to hold her forever but instead he let her go almost at once. They stood apart.

'Merry Christmas,' he said.

After kissing him lightly on the cheek, she went out of the main door. Frank watched her go and then made his way back through the store to leave by another exit. As Molly walked on down Fifth Avenue, he came out into 56th Street. They walked steadily away through the crowd, at right angles to each other.

The gap between them widened in every sense.

169

Molly was badly shaken. She had prayed that she would see him again and yet the experience had left her jangled. Instead of explaining things to him, she had further confused him. Instead of drawing closer to him, she felt that she had pushed him away. Instead of telling him that she was now effectively a free woman, she let him believe that she was still living with Brian in Ardsley. She stopped. An urge to go back seized her. But it evaporated as soon as she asked herself what she was going to say and do. He had his wife and his children and his job in Houston. He did not need her.

Frank's need, in fact, had never been more painful. It caused him to halt in a doorway and look back towards Rizzoli's. Should he run back after her and tell her what he was really feeling? The idea died at birth. She had made it quite clear during their brief chat in the bookstore that their affair was firmly in the past. She had been uncomfortable with him. Frank had started to tell her that he and Ann had separated but the words had stuck in his throat.

He began walking again and came to a stoplight at an intersection. The sign changed from DON'T WALK to WALK. Frank obeyed.

Molly, too, was at a stoplight. For her also, the sign changed from DON'T WALK to WALK.

It seemed like a command. DON'T WALK AWAY. WALK TOGETHER.

Tears streamed down Molly's face. Frank fought hard to maintain control of his emotions. The distance between them grew. They were walking steadily out of each other's lives.

Clock chimes suddenly rang out. Molly consulted her watch, saw that it was time to go and stepped off the kerb.

'Taxi! Taxi!'

Frank had stopped in his tracks. People pushed and

jostled him but he did not move. His eyes were fixed on the clock face high above him. It was six-fifteen. The chimes were ringing out his last chance. Molly's voice whispered in his ear.

'You can't live without hope . . .'

He flung himself into the road and flagged down a taxi.

'Where to, buddy?'

'Grand Central. Go like hell!'

'In this traffic?'

The station was a babble of noise and confusion as thousands headed home for their Christmas. Molly had to fight her way to her gate and then she was borne along by the crowd to the platform. The train seemed to be packed with more and more passengers climbing aboard. Molly hesitated. She wanted to go back but knew that it would be too late. She wanted someone to stop her but that someone was not there. She remained on the platform until the very last moment and then reluctantly she stepped on the train. Doors slid into position. The engine stirred and they were in motion.

There were no seats anywhere and Molly had to stand between the cars. Even there she was subjected to an unpleasant crush as other passengers pressed up against her. She had never seen the train so full before and yet, in her mind, so empty. The journey home would be an ordeal in every way and when she got to the house, the ordeal would continue. No welcome. No warmth. No company. Nothing.

Christmas alone. Without love. Without value.

Without hope.

She glanced down the car and saw that several passengers were having to stand in the aisle, supporting themselves by holding the backs of the seats. Molly was about to turn away when something caught her attention. A man

171

was making his way along the car, squeezing with difficulty past human obstacles. All that she could see of him was the top of his head, but it was enough. She struggled to find a small space.

Frank came out of the car. When their eyes met, no more words were necessary. She flung herself into his arms and he hugged her as tightly as he could. Their kiss was a seal on the future.

They would never have to live without hope again.

The train thundered on through the night.

Bestsellers available in Panther Books

Emmanuelle Arsan

Emmanuelle	£1.95	☐
Emmanuelle 2	£1.95	☐
Laure	£1.50	☐
Nea	£1.50	☐
Vanna	£1.95	☐
The Secrets of Emmanuelle (non-fiction)	95p	☐

Jonathan Black

Ride the Golden Tiger	£1.95	☐
Oil	£1.95	☐
The World Rapers	£1.95	☐
The House on the Hill	£1.95	☐
Megacorp	£2.50	☐
The Plunderers	£2.50	☐

Herbert Kastle

Cross-Country	£1.95	☐
Little Love	£1.95	☐
Millionaires	£1.95	☐
Miami Golden Boy	£1.95	☐
The Movie Maker	£2.50	☐
The Gang	£1.95	☐
Hit Squad	£1.95	☐
Dirty Movies	£1.95	☐
Hot Prowl	£1.50	☐
Sunset People	£1.95	☐
David's War	£1.95	☐

To order direct from the publisher just tick the titles you want
and fill in the order form.

Bestsellers available in Panther Books

Sverre Holm
I, a Man   £1.50 ☐

Sixtus Holm
I, a Missionary   95p ☐

Morgan Holm
I, a Sailor   £1.50 ☐

Nina Holm
I, a Prostitute   £1.50 ☐

Siv Holm
I, a Woman   £1.25 ☐

Susanne Holm
I, Susanne   £1.25 ☐

Tine Holm
I, a Teenager   95p ☐

Grania Beckford
Touch the Fire   £2.50 ☐
Catch the Fire   £1.95 ☐

Xaviera Hollander
Lucinda, my Lovely   £1.95 ☐

To order direct from the publisher just tick the titles you want
and fill in the order form.

All these books are available at your local bookshop or newsagent, or can be ordered direct from the publisher.

To order direct from the publisher just tick the titles you want and fill in the form below.

Name _____

Address _____

_____